Jean Giono

The Serpent of Stars

Translated by Jody Gladding

archipelago books

Library of Congress Cataloging-in-Publication Data
Giono, Jean, 1895–1970.
[Le Serpent d'étoiles. English]
The serpent of stars / Jean Giono ; translated by Jody Gladding.
p. cm.
ISBN 0-9728692-8-X
I. Gladding, Jody, 1955–ꞏ II. Title.
PQ2613.I57S413 2004
843'.912–dc22   2003023998

Publication of this translation was assisted
by a grant from the French Ministry of Culture –
Centre National du Livre.

Archipelago Books
New York, New York
www.archipelagobooks.org

Distributed by
Consortium Book Sales and Distribution
1045 Westgate Drive
St. Paul, Minnesota 55114
www.cbsd.com

Contents

I first read *The Serpent of Stars* in France in 1998. First published in 1933, it was out of print at that time, but I found a copy of the fifth printing (1949) at a used book stand at the market in Apt. The pages were still uncut. I am deeply indebted to Elizabeth Deshays, first for recommending the book, and then for reading through and repairing my translation of it. I would also like to thank M. Dumas, of the Dumas Bookstore in Apt, for serving as consultant. It is to them I owe the following anecdote.

When the composer Darius Milhaud read this novel, he loved it, and curious about the extraordinary, unknown musical instruments described in it, he wrote to Giono to find out more about them. Giono wrote a laconic note back saying that he couldn't tell him anything more about them, simply because he had made them up.

All the footnotes in this text are also Giono's inventions. As translator, I've added none of my own.

To Professor Eduard Wechssler

Can your performance face the open fields and the seaside?

WALT WHITMAN

The Serpent of Stars

I

It ALL BEGAN WITH CÉSAIRE ESCOFFIER. It all began that May day. The sky was smooth as a washing stone; the mistral had scrubbed it blue; the sun spurted out from all sides; things no longer had shadows; the mystery was there, against the skin; this wind of perdition tore words from the lips and carried them off into other worlds. Despite all that, "you did the fair." You can hardly give up a fair in May. If rain threatens, you take along an umbrella. If this wind comes up, you hurl yourself into it like a swimmer, you thrash about like a mill with arms, you bellow out the prices, you spend the whole day with your eyes shut, your ears ruptured, as if in a sea, but even so, you do business, and in the evening, sheltered by the walls, you open your eyelids, burned by the salt and the wind. Your bag of coins, like something ripped from the sea bottom, is full of bits of grass and sand.

That was when I went looking for the shepherds. Usually I found them near the blanket merchant buying themselves what they needed for life on the plateaus. This time, I didn't find their cart and the edge-toolmaker told me, "He didn't come. He took cold in the mountain passes. We were all together at the Laragne fair. We left in the middle of the night. It got to him in no time at all. 'It seems as though I'm breathing knives,' he said to me. He's up there at the inn by the road, Au Panier des Filles, do you know it?"

That took the wind out of my sails! No more shepherds! No more fair this time around! I had counted on today, hoping I might learn the rest of that epic, "The Evergreen Oaks"! It was as though I was in a dream and unable to think. I drew away into those sheltered alleyways: the Observantine and the Aubette where the wind makes more peaceful lakes.

There the honeysuckle on the houses barely moved, pools of silence and shadow slept in the curve of the walls. This was at street level beyond the wind's reach, a country where you always have to be on your guard.

After a little while, in this bay between the grocery and the boat captain's house, I saw gleaming on the cobblestones what looked like a stream of little stars. It ran under a large arbor of roses. I let myself get used to the darkness; the coolness and calm of the street poured into my open eyes like the good black water of sleep. At my feet, I saw a whole herd of gleaming pots, and the potter was looking at me.

There were olive jars, tea pots, water jugs, and a great paunch of sweaty black clay for the man to use. He had just finished drinking. He wiped his mustache. He was also made of clay.

FROM ALL sides, the sly day shifted about; and the mistral shook the sky like sheet metal.

In the middle of the pots, in a square marked off by cords of red wool, arranged in three rows, there were little pot-bellied pots, stuffed with newspaper. I thought of the honey from the hills and I said to the man, "You must give me one of those."

"Are you in love?" he asked in response.

It reached me at the same time as his blue gaze, soft and amenable as underwater grass, and the sudden mystery of the day pure of shadows.

Should I say yes? No? How to find the truth in that!

I explained, "I'm married, and so . . ."

He asked, "Is your wife sick?"

I quickly said no, because all of a sudden, I had understood. It all tied in: the alleyway resonant as a large flute, this diluted sun, this sky so thick that its color ran over the outline of the houses, this clay man gifted with speech: it was all a spell!

WE SEALED a good, strong friendship, not over a glass of anise at the Café de la Boscotte, but like that, without moving from our spots, him over there, me here on the other side of the pots and our looks exchanging between them more and more of his blue and my blue of friendship.

In the end, he stepped over all his mute clay, he reached out his tree root of a hand, all rough; he said, "If you have the time, come see me. Judging from what you were about to say, we'll get along fine together. My name is Césaire Escoffier."

· ·

HE HAD explained very clearly to me that he lived in Saint-Martin-l'Eau, that you first had to go to the village, then take a left after the threshing ground with all the bales of wheat, then climb to the spine of the Berre hut, then cross through the pine woods, then look for the bloody wound of his clay pit in the hill. When I reached the jostling rush of hills, my heart began to sink. Such waves of earth and spray of trees as far as the eye could see! A big ivy squatting in the hollow of the valley was gnawing the fleshless bones of a dead farm. It swung its heavy head. It tossed its green suckers in the grass; it went off in its slow desire, heavy with branches and black leaves, toward a groaning sheepfold. The earth was torn up by great claws; in other places, it was beaten and trampled like a wallow, but all along its width and length it retained the imprint of some beast heavier than the sky. Apart from that, there was no sign of a bird, no squeal of rats in the bushes, or that sound of a spring big snakes make when they flow sleepily through the grass. There was only the life of sap, but all of it so hot with life you felt that ferocious burning just by touching the light stem of a honeysuckle.

I am used to it, but I stood there facing it a good while, naked and cold. Finally, I got up my courage and I went down into the foam of the trees. By noon I was wandering lost, my throat on fire, in this prison of a valley that forms the base of a huge crater. Where to turn when, with each step, a tree moves, scolding you from behind? Three times already, separating the branches of apple trees grown wild, I had seen a solid wall of rock behind them. The sun had sucked out all my moisture. I was dry as dead wood hearing my skin crack, my brain doing red cartwheels in the blackness of my head, when I heard the sound of a three-tone flute, completely human, so very human, so human that with the rest of my moisture, I let out an "Oh!" full of hope. The flute fell silent.

After a moment, it sounded further on, near the willows of an abandoned drinking trough. I went there. No one! Just water which leaped in fits and starts out of the wooden spout, water heavy with the smell of sulfur, water so thick with earth that it had filled its basin with yellow mud and was overflowing it.

The flute rang out from under the pines. In its direction I found an opening between two rocks. Struggling desperately with the serpents of an elder tree, I passed through. There were seeds, bits of flowers in my hair; a big sticky leaf clung to my cheek. But, emerging like that when you've lost hope, your courage quickly returns. The path was there beneath my feet; the flute rang out there ahead of me like a hunting dog's bell. I walked, the trees withdrew from my road, the grass was cool against my legs, and all of a sudden I saw, above, on the hillside, a deep wound, dark from bleeding clay.

"So!" he called, seeing me arrive, "you come from below? You look like a human plant. Whatever possessed you?"

He waited for me above his clearing, and drawn by his large hand which had grasped my own, I made the last step. He gave me the two-spouted jug. I replenished myself with water inside and out by pouring it down my throat, by spraying my chest with its clear rays. After that, I felt a breath of wind. Everything returned to order in my head, and it seemed to me that I was still the master.

I MIGHT as well say at once how strange this dwelling place was. In the hills, a current of water is life. The place knows it so well that it remains there, arid and dry, motionless, sure of its old powers, its burning ground, its blurry air, like flames in which those broad illusions of mirage silently explode. A current of water passes under the nostrils, and you're saved. As for me, I just had the entire hand of water caressing me. It was still there curling my hairs in its cool fingers. I had become the master of my body once again when, before following Césaire, who said to me, "Come to the workshop," I gazed all around, from the distant depths of the sky to the thick dappled meadow that kept the spring water folded safely within its leaves.

BELOW US the brush, like a swamp with its thick odor of rotting grass, went off on its foaming way to rest against the far horizon of blue iron. This tip of the hill emerged like a small island; a great cavern, black and bloody as a hole in live flesh, was the home of Escoffier.

Within, against the daylight of the doorway, two wheels were set up: one large one for a man to use, one small one for I don't know what, so miniature it immediately conjured a light body made of air and thought. On the shelf was another one of those little magic pots.

"You see," he said to me, "she was just making it."

"Who?" I said, my eyes wide, not daring to move my feet for fear of stepping on her.

"My daughter, the eldest, the redhead. She's the one who invented everything. There you have it. I believe that it came from a dream she had. She began to turn that from the hollow of her thumb. The teacher told me, 'She doesn't do anything, she yawns if I talk, it's as if she was drawn out of another world and she's still watching that other world through a little hole.' 'Her eyes are completely empty, your daughter's.' So, I said, 'Okay, she'll stay at home.' It's true, she has the eyes of a goat. So one evening, I talked it over with her. We were lying down under the pines. She was stretched out against my side, her head resting on my arm. She said 'Papa!' I said, 'Yes, my girl!'

"But I'm making you stand there and you've just had a long walk. Have a seat, we'll just wait for you to stop sweating, and then I'll introduce you to my family. You'll stay with us tonight, we've got a place for you to sleep. You don't mind sleeping on the ground?"

We were there on the front bench, a bit of evening was beginning to rise up in the woods, and already its calm water, rocked in the base of the crater, was engulfing the holm oaks. The earth sighed a long sigh, so soft, so calm that no more than two or three eddies of birds rose. The wild swallows called to one another. All together they dove from the top of the sky toward our two human faces. They were like bits of dead wood in a great whirlpool. The ocean of sky rolled over us in the peaceful life of its waves. We were there in the depths of that great brine of all life, at the very source of truth in life's thick mud, which is the mixture of men, beasts, trees, and rock. Under the palm of my hand, I felt the slow pulse of granite, I heard the currents of sap carrying their loads; my blood throbbed in my head, and coming from the boundaries of the sky, powerful rushes of cold and heat brushed my cheeks as if from a thrown stone.

The sun remained perched like a pigeon on our summit. This meadow which protected the spring extended further than the waters. From the grass where she was taking an afternoon nap, the mistress of the pottery rose with the rush of the wind.

"My wife," said Césaire.

She was white and soft, and fat, completely covered with fat, so much fat, so soft that you expected to see her arms suddenly pour out of the barrels of her sleeves like mortar. Her lovely full, round head laughed the eternal laugh of the moon. Her beautiful black, well-groomed hair, glistening with pure oil, smelled of olive and fennel. Her eyes were as big as green almonds. She stood up. And immediately one, two, three, four, five children began to pour from her like a spray of seeds, like drops of spring water. Suddenly there she was, in the grass, like a spring rushing with children, and the last to detach herself from her—frail, red-haired, milky and salty as an April morning—was that young sorceress with gentian eyes.

These were the gestures, natural and simple. We made a meal of grass and night. On the edge of the clearing was set down a large plate full of this salad of the hills, very pale, picked in the shade, wriggling about, gleaming with oil, like a nest of green spiders. We dug in with our fingers, each in turn. We were all in a circle, with the plate in the middle. A large slab of bread in the left hand served as plate and napkin, and when that bread had soaked up enough oil, had wiped the fingers well enough, we ate it, and it tasted like a harvest afternoon.

The night we munched with the salad. The night overflowed from the crater in slow gushes, and our mouths were full of night when we bit into the bread crusts rubbed with garlic. So we had those grasses to eat, and then the night—and it was a night in the brush, and then, those strange yellow glances from the fourteen-year-old witch. It all provided food for the belly and the brain. I don't know if the brain really had its separate share. I think rather that everything, salad, oil, dark bread, night, and the gentian glances, they all went into the belly, there they all made weight and warmth, there they were all changed into saps and smells, so much so that finally, we were drunk from the triple power of the sky, the earth, and truth.

TWICE already I had heard that sound of the cowbell, once near the pine forest which slept growling like a sheep dog, the other time near that crouching white rock, liquid as a weasel when it moves, and now I heard it again and I looked up at a big red star.

"The shepherd will be with us," said Escoffier. "Woman, chill the hyssop water."

The children's bed had been laid out: a thick, creaking layer of dried grass. They were on top of it, completely naked, sprawled out, arms and legs tangled, scraping bellies, slapping bottoms, the force of their movements releasing the scents of savory and citronella. I heard them say, "We haven't killed the lion!"

"Poor thing! Let it sleep a little first."

"The sun's out."

"It's the sun of the rain."

"There's only one sun."

"There's the right sun and the left sun."

AND THE shepherd arrived at the same time as the moon. No, the moon had arrived first. It was there, rising slowly over the roundness of the opposite hill, when the shepherd came noiselessly out of the lower valley, and he obliterated the moon with his huge body.

"Company, Césaire and everyone," he said, "so, how are you?"

"Fine," said Césaire, "as you can see, we're enjoying this fine night."

A moment ago, the young sorceress had undressed at the same time as her brothers and sisters; I had heard snaps click, and then she shed her dress like a skin, throwing it off her shoulders, shaking it from the ends of her arms, freeing her legs one after the other from that fallen thing. From over there she cried, "Oh, shepherd!"

Then she came, without shame in front of the men, and for all we could see, her whole body smooth as a washed stone.

We were there, on the edge of the clearing, on a moon beach. A big night beetle's shell made the empty salad bowl ring as it scrabbled with its huge forehead and mad feet against the slippery curve of the earthenware. We could hear ourselves breathe. The wind was hot, then cool, according to whether it brought in the hollow of its hand the round air from the depths of the valleys or the air flat as a knife sharpened on the millstone of the high moors. Each time the beetle's armature sounded in the empty bowl, the almond eyes of the pottery's mistress gazed long at her naked daughter, then at Césaire and the shepherd, and I saw her white mouth, which was attempting silent words. The shepherd, a man of about fifty, big of bone but not heavy with flesh, without anything more than dry leather skin over leather muscles, a man of the hills, made of sun, dust, and dead leaves, the shepherd, sitting on the hard ground, facing the night, played around on a big nine-pipe flute with his fingers; he tapped out a little tune, scratching the sensitive pipes with the ends of his fingernails.

All this was difficult, as much for Césaire as for the shepherd as for the wise little girl. You could feel it, they were like big balloons full of a thick wine. And the mother only removed the cork after looking hard at me. Here I was, simpler and more fragile than fleabane. All the winds battered me, and I had just heard the thick gravel of the sky rolling in this silence when she said, "And you, mister, you know how to sleep on a grass bed in our earthen home?"

"Yes," I said, completely overcome, and then, "yes, this won't be the first time. I often do it. And I love the coolness of caves and that warmth you get, come morning, and then, Césaire, shepherd, let's not put on airs, this is our true home, in fact, beneath it all."

Little by little, equilibrium and ease returned to me. I had only to show my heart to these men, to these women, and I was sure of being loved, and I was sure of understanding all their thoughts, of being at the source of their reflections, of being their very selves, neither more fat, nor less fat, of being with them and emerging from the grass no more than they did, healthy beasts among the grasses and the beasts.

"Yes," said the wife, "but, Césaire, don't put him near the root."

"What root?" I said. "What do you mean a root?"

"The root of a tree," said the woman, "a white root. It's there bulging from the ground like running milk, but it's hard and full of ill will, you can't imagine. And it's sly and impossibly strong, and once it tried to wrap itself around my foot and it was going to draw me down to the bottom of the earth."

"There you go again with your root," said Césaire, his voice slow and true as he turned his head, and then he drifted off into the night once more on the beautiful wings of his gaze.

The young witch had wrapped her soft dress around her waist. The shepherd hummed quietly like a spring. The children were asleep, you could hear them sleeping, and there was the moon, over the hilly heap of naked children.

"Let me, Césaire, let me talk. On the other side of the wall, when we were at the inn in Lincel, you remember, Césaire, a house above ground. There were two charcoal burners, a man and a woman who was his wife. We heard them living. On the other side of the wall, there was a block of day or a block of night and human life. We heard him, the man, when he slapped her like a mill with arms, slapped all that was only skin and bones and rang like an empty barrel. 'Oh, sweet Jesus,' she said, 'this savage is going to kill me!' A little later, she was laughing and they began fooling around so noisily that I said to that one... (she pointed to the young redhead), 'Sleep, close your eyes, it's none of your business what they're up to.'

"And then they were snoring, which wasn't hard to imagine and was no cause for fear. There you have it. In the morning, the man would walk out, ho hum, swinging his carbide lantern, whistling that song of the Piémont, and with the first notes I said to you, 'Césaire, wake up, he's whistling, listen, isn't it beautiful.' And the woman, that was easy to imagine, too. She would come down the stairs about the time I would be sitting by the fountain combing my hair. She would come down the stairs, heavy with a big bundle of dirty laundry in her arms, and she would stop from time to time to pull up her slipping stocking, and she would come and throw it all into the washing basin, and then standing up again, she would say, 'Ouf! That's enough to keep me busy today.' Yes, whatever is human I can imagine, and I do like to go off into those lives that aren't mine and follow them a bit, and then leave them when things become difficult, and come back into the life of my body, which is what it is, but it's mine. I like that well enough and so I don't need to be afraid. But as for what happens behind the walls of the earth, that I don't like, but it's stronger than me, it draws me in and it sucks me under and it drinks me."

She stopped for a moment to lick her lips with her big, quick tongue.

"Here," she went on, "you could say that I have the bread and the knife, but I like the bitterness of it; it makes my brain water, you might say. I've spent a long time listening to the sound of the earth and I've always listened to the neighbors, but here, the neighbors, well, first of all, it's those huge gray pines and then those fine old oaks as thick as men, with human voices but so heavy with a power that comes from the depths of time, so that you say to yourself, 'If they wanted to . . . !' And at first, I lay down against the right wall. And there, all at once, as soon as I stretched out on my bed, I was plunged into sleep, like a candle blown out. A thing that blew out my life all at once. One night, I struggled with my eyelids. They lowered, I lifted them, until I had to hold them open with my fingertips. There was a purring, like a cat's, in the earth's big throat. And I was going into this noise, saying to myself, 'It's that, or that, or maybe it's that!' until the moment when I saw the black life of a spring, and I said, 'Césaire, I'm making my bed over there, you can come if you like, and if you stay, there'll be no more children, because I tell you I'm not leaving that left side anymore. My mother didn't make me for sleeping beside a spring that never sleeps.' And Césaire came because he has to be against a woman's flesh, that's his nature.

(Césaire is still out in the night; the wife wets her lips.)

". . . There, one fine evening, I heard scratching for a long time. It made a *tock*, and a bit of earth fell on the blanket and from the hole, a long white root came out. Ever since, it's grown, it twists itself and twists again. Luckily, it's blind. It's searching for me.

"It was a summer evening, and the big door was opened wide onto the night. That one lay down beside me and put her little arm around my neck. That was no good because I have a big neck and I'm heavy, and I said to her, 'Move your arm, I'll hurt you,' but she stayed close to me and I was frozen with fear and she was hot as a coal burning me where she clung. And she said to me, 'Mama, look at the night. It's full of stars someone's only just sown. Who is it who sows them? Who is it who has a sack full of them? It's fistfuls and fistfuls that someone throws. They look like rice, look.'

"She talked without stopping, all hot with her heat. And I slept with her little arm around me."

IT WAS now the middle of the night. Madame Escoffier's voice was slow and heavy like mortar, like the mortar of her flesh. I saw her again hardly two weeks ago, and I thought about all the bends and turns of that night as I tossed in my hands the large fruit picked at the end of the road. And I was drawn back to the clay cave and to my friends. In Lincel, in Saint-Martin-les-Eaux, you wouldn't know that this fat woman with the beautiful children knows the countries beyond the air. When she goes off to do her shopping in Forcalquier, if she examines the egg-plant, if she squeezes the artichoke, you don't know, you couldn't know, that she is knowledgeable in the great science of sky and earth, that she knows, according to the very deepest secrets, the eggplant's true weight and the artichoke's bitter blood.

At that hour, it was the middle of the night, night thick with uncut leaves, beautiful night slapping like a sail, sea blue night, and its wave rolled onto the beach of trees, into those reefs of the hills' summits. The moon's spray broke gently against the rocks.

Césaire grabbed me by the wrist and, without thinking, drew me to him with his rough strength, and I felt the great pincers of his fingers enter my flesh.

"SO," HE SAID, brusquely and between his teeth, "now you know, now you've heard the woman. Do we understand each other or not? . . ."

Suddenly my head was full of all those emotions raised by trees, that great love for bark, that friendship with boughs, and also that fear before the motionless sway of their overwhelming life, everything that, since my youth and my first steps into the hills, inhabited me, and I answered straight from the heart, "Yes, we understand each other, we were made to understand each other, this must have been destined long ago."

"Speaking of that," said the wife . . .

But the shepherd raised his hand in the moonlight and began to speak.

As I've said, this was a dry man, made of a pile of scree. He spoke with a dark creaking. His mouth opened into his beard and the words came out from between teeth all healthy and ice white despite his age.

"In the rock of Volx, there are tawny eagles. If you lie down in the grass, they come. They turn into the wind, there overhead, and then they dive straight down. The eagle's shadow wakes you. If you're asleep, it passes cool over your eyelids, and you wake up. There it is. You wake up, even if you're sleeping well.

"Once, I had a dog. He was mean as the wind. He didn't know what he did anymore than the wind does. He passed over everything, brutal, all his strength concentrated. He cowed a Corsican ram as big as a load of hay. It was the sheared ewes that killed him. They revolted. They smothered him, then trampled him to death. Then they came to see me, contrite. And I said, 'Good!'

"Once I saw someone, a man, a child I should say—I saw someone who carried the weight of the sky. His whole back trembled from it and he bellowed like a bull because he didn't know how to talk, because he had never known how to talk to men. And the birds all came from across the fields. The birds and all the beasts, but the first day, it was only the birds, that first day, he had a bird on the tip of each of his fingers.

"I knew a man called Martial of Reillanne who had the curse of the beast upon him. Dogs, cats, horses, sheep, anything; at the scent of him, they all went mad. He wanted to try an experiment. He bought a horse at the Mane fair. It was his wife who led the horse; he was walking at least a hundred meters behind, but when the woman touched the snaffle with her left hand, the horse raised its head and clacked its teeth against the bit. It was because the woman touched her husband with this left hand at night. When the horse was in the stable, Martial said, 'I have to see. Maybe it's this jacket that I'm wearing.' He took off the jacket. Then on down, he took off his belt, his breeches, his shoes. He got completely naked, and he said, 'Just in case! . . . Like this, I'll really be able to tell.' It was no use. He went into the stable naked. The horse smashed its hoofs rearing against the stone wall. Everything died from disgust: chickens, ducks, rabbits. It got worse and worse. One day, he was leaving a café, and a pigeon flew over his head, beat its wings, and rolled over dead. He looked at the bird and said, 'That's it.' He went to find a rope and he hung himself. He walked through the whole village with his rope. Nobody stopped him.

"There are trees and there are animals. I was a small-time boss, a small-time shepherd. Two hundred sheep. My proprietor lived in Raphèle. Two hundred sheep, it's not many, not enough to understand.

"There are great bosses, there are big-time shepherds. In charge of ten thousand beasts, a hundred thousand beasts, masters who open the door, say only one word into the darkness of each sheepfold. The great wooden gates are opened wide, the hired hands are there lined up on either side. And the boss says the word, just one, no more, then he turns his back, tightens his hand around his staff and he sets off, and the sheep come out, and the sheep walk behind him. It's like a sash that he's attached to his sides and that he unravels over the country. He walks along ahead, he sets off, he draws the sheep. They fall into step, they start walking. He is already over there in the far distance, having crossed through two or three villages, two or three woods, two or three hills. He is like the needle and the whole thread of sheep passes where he has passed. It passes through the villages, the woods, the hills behind him. Here, the sheep are still leaving the stable. Ten thousand, a hundred thousand, that's quite a stretch. As they go along, the assistants who are there with the hired hands say, 'Good-bye, it's my turn,' and one after the other, they set off. The last sheep goes out, the stable is closed. It goes out of the yard, the big gates are closed. No one watches. It's a mystery. Above the wall, the dust rises. You hear that sound of a big stream, a big herd, that sound of the world, that sound of sky, that sound of stars. It's a mystery. The proprietor takes off his hat. He feels small with all his paper deeds housed at the lawyer's office. That isn't what makes a master. He thinks of the needle that draws the long thread of sheep. He says, 'Come, let's have a drink,' and everyone goes into the kitchen.

"Those others are the great masters of the beasts; they are the ones that know."

THAT WAS how the night proceeded, and now I felt it all damp, stuck against the round of earth like a sheet coming out of the wash. The moon had taken on its full speed; a little spray of cloud escaped from under its sinking weight. I remembered my tremendous youth, that time when, by whatever divination, I had been delivered over to the great powers, in confidence, with the words, "Here's the child, take him." Now I understood that great blue gaze of my father's when, returning from those summer months when I had followed after Massot the shepherd, pale from the green of the grass and emitting the scent of fennel, I entered the workshop where he had remained crouched over. So it wasn't the health of the flesh that he felt in me when, seizing me by the shoulders, he planted me in front of him to look, before embracing me. It was the health of the spirit. "And now, you know, son?"

That was how the night proceeded. We were on the rooftops of the world.

Césaire breathed in the four corners of the sky.

"There's the wind," he said, "there's our wind, shepherd. We're going to be able to play."

In the quick of the moon, in that circle of short grass embraced by the woods, a beautiful pine lyre held up its two trunks.

As you approached, the tree began to sing in a voice that was human and vegetable at the same time. I saw that someone had harnessed the two horns of the tree by means of a hollow yoke. They had extended nine cords from the yoke to the foot of the tree. Thus, it had become a living lyre, full all at once with the ample life of the wind, the mute life of the trunks swollen with resin, and the blood-gorged life of man.

The shepherd touched the cords to adjust them. You could hear the sounds falling far below, in the middle of the brush, and the leaves muttered, as though under large raindrops from a storm. Finally, the shepherd stood with his back against the huge curved trunk, he spread his hands wide to span the strings, and he waited for the wind.

We heard it. Beyond the valleys, the wide plateaus were already whistling under it like hot iron dipped in water. It arrived.

It arrived, and immediately, from the level height of the hill soared the song of the three lives. The whole tree vibrated all the way down to its roots, and with the wide reach of his fingers, the man gripped the reins of that beautiful flying horse. The whole sky streamed through the lyre. Then a hailstorm of birds fell from the night, and, like stones on the move, the sheep began to climb up through the woods.

They emerged quietly from the line of trees. They came, step by step, one by one, without a sound. There they were, heads lowered, listening, and rams' horns dragged in the grass, and trembling all over, the lamb hid under its mother's belly.

Without a sound!

Only once in a while, deep in the grass, the beasts sighed, all together. The hills fell silent. The man gave a voice to the joy and the sadness of the world.

II

A PRISON OF FOUR WALLS AND A whole cemetery of books, but, sometimes, those walls draw apart, open, like a huge flower, and a deluge of sky crashes down inside there in a rush.

When you carry away with you the words "masters of beasts," and the mute music of the pine-lyre, you are no longer the man you were before. You have taken a step toward the countries beyond the air; you are already beyond the air. The ordinary world passes just against your back. Before you opens the wide plain of clouds, and all your skin expands under the suction of those unknown lands.

I have always remembered how that night ended. Dawn came. I knew it because the eyes of the sheep all went out at the same time. The moon sank behind the darkness.

"Let's take advantage of the good hours," said Césaire.

The wind died. The last note flew off all alone like the dove from the ark.

The wife gathered the cluster of children. She took them off into the clay cave. The young sorceress woke her brother, the next oldest after her, and she dragged him along, pulling him by the hand, him lagging heavily behind, his head hanging, his eyes closed, her, lean as a bone, with those living antennae, her yellow eyes.

I said, "I'll sleep outside with the shepherd."

Yes, I was afraid of the root and that spring from the depths of the earth. The shepherd lent me a homespun coat, tight at the collar, but then full around the body, and, folded within that wool which smelled of mule and thick grass, I was going off to sleep when the man leaned over me, with his white face, and said, "When you come back, I will tell you what I did the night of the great revolt."

. .

THEN CAME the time of the summer solstice. The desire was constantly within me like a caper bush, beautiful flowers, but thorns and a taste of pepper to make you salivate like a fountain. Tired of the inner turmoil all that created, I took up my walking stick. That act alone was magic. It was a ritual gesture. A great wave of smells rushed over me. The wind took me by the shoulders like a sail and I set off from the coast of Saint-Martin-l'Eau.

First of all, I have to say that lots of things gave me impetus that day. In the morning, first, I heard a large herd enter the town from the south and grate against the houses as it crammed the streets. I went to wait for them at the fountains. The shepherds were wild-eyed. The head shepherd jumped out from all sides like a grasshopper giving orders which, at hearing them, you sat down, mouth open. Only the dogs went to stretch out in the shade. They watered the sheep. They gave them a little rest, standing, not letting them fold their legs or lie down, then "Hup!" The head shepherd whistled through his fingers and they all set off with their sleepiness and their suffering.

After that, I was watching peacefully from my window which looks out over everything, and there I saw it: the whole county was smoking under the hooves of the sheep. From Pertuis, from Valensole, from Pierrevert, from Corbières, from Sainte-Tulle, the lead sheep nudged one another on along the roads in the full fire of the great sun. Already, in the background, the Durance was lying in a cloud of earth thicker than the clouds of the sky, and the sound of a spring that had released all its waters danced over the country like a huge serpent crushing all the foliage.

It was the height of the move to summer pastures. All the animals left the red Crau, where the full sun was already crushing everything.

So, in the hills at noon, I ate my bread at the Turpine spring and I stayed there for an hour to watch the water fleas jumping. That noise of animals on the move was constantly in the sky. It resounded across the clouds as if across stretched skin. The noise no longer rose from the earth. A gray haze which was the dust from the fields and roads poured across the sky in the slow curves of thick, beautiful muscles. The whole world took part in the emigration of the beasts. The order had come from beyond the sky in the dazzling mystery of the sun. The rising tide of beasts obeyed the world's orders. I was filled with that great monotonous noise like a sponge in a basin. I was more that noise than myself.

The streams of sheep descended the length of my arms. I heard them gathering in the great woods of my hair. Their horned feet sounded heavily against the full of my chest. All of a sudden, I felt the dizzying rotation of the earth and I woke up.

Already that lovely silence, already that edge of evening, and the cowbell of the poor shepherd rang over there from under the blue junipers.

He let me get my breath beside him, and then he handed me his water jug. I saw that he, too, had his natural home there, not like the potter's, who hollows out the earth and then kneads it, knowing the forms, but only goes that far, without knowing what spirit to breathe into it. No, this was the home of the master, the pine-lyre player, the initiated who listens to the words of the clouds and reads the great writing of the stars: a hut of loosely woven branches, ethereal, saturated with air.

THIS IS what he told me:

I was fifteen years old. In the middle of winter, the master felt my arms. He said, "Let me see your legs." I lifted my pants. He passed his hands over my legs and felt my calves. "Good," he said, "you'll leave for the Alps this spring, but first, show me your teeth." I rolled back my lips like a laughing dog, and he said, "Alright," and this time, it was decided. First I went to say good-bye to my team of horses, and then I went to find the shepherds. They were camping in the hayloft, on the fine hay, humpbacked as the open sea. Like all young shepherds, I stayed there to test the waters, and in the evening, instead of sleeping under the stairs as I usually did, I dug myself a burrow in the hay to sleep beside them.

At Christmas, we went to the church to welcome Jesus, and I wasn't among the plowboys, but with the team of shepherds. I'd been lent a sheepskin jacket, a pointed hat, and a fife. Coming out, old Bouscarle put his hand on my shoulder. "Jesus," he said to me, "is up there." And as I looked at the vast sky, he said to me, "No, not in the vastness, in that little corner, there, you see, that tiny star."

Bouscarle was my boss. He was the one who gave me some idea of all you had to know to be an assistant shepherd, and especially, to take care of the beasts. "Look after them," he would say to me, "but the most important thing is to win their trust. Every movement you make must be true. Maintain your balance. When you're carrying a big bowl full of water, you don't run."

You've slept in good thick hay once in a while, haven't you? Then you know that after two nights, you aren't the same anymore. It gets you as drunk as brandy. Every morning, Bouscarle put his outstretched hand on my head and looked me in the eye. "You resist, son," he would say to me, "you resist; that's no good." And in fact, I'll admit to you that I did resist that drunkenness of the grass with all my strength. But the grass is stronger than anything because its days are endless and because, from the beginning of time and until the end, it has always wanted the same thing. And one fine morning, Bouscarle looked me straight in the eye without saying anything. I saw a shadow of a smile in the dark of his beard. That afternoon, he led me to the sheep. He opened the door of the stable; he shut it again behind us, and there we stood motionless in the shadows. He gave me no advice that day. I did everything as though someone else was doing it through me. The odor of beasts was a great thing for raising fear.

After a moment, we began to see more clearly in there. A little daylight came through a round window, through the cobwebs. A large hornet swam softly around the stable, effortlessly, carried on the thickness of all that breathing. Bouscarle said one word. All the heads of the sheep turned toward us. In the faint light from the window, the beasts' eyes began to gleam like stars in the night, and it seemed like I could hear their brains jostling in their skulls.

"Jesus," said Bouscarle, "is the smallest of all the gods. A shepherd, nothing but a shepherd. First, there was the one whose body we all were, before becoming pieces of it. Jesus was a bigger piece than the others, that's all. There are big gods, my boy, and those are the ones you're going to have to get used to."

As we were going out, Bouscarle said, "Come, I'm going to teach you to play the fife."

We had to go out to the big strawshed in the open fields, and there, just the two of us played far into the night. He showed me how to place my fingers over the holes. And I tried as hard as I could, but the joints of my fingers needed oiling, and sometimes I let up too soon, sometimes too late. Then he had me learn the art of breathing. First he blew and then he passed the flute, all warm, to me and on the willow reed I tasted garlic and wine, the breath of Bouscarle. The first notes went well, because the shepherd's breath was still in the flute, and then I was left on my own, alone in a void emptier than the great void of the sea, and it was hard to raise it, the weight of the music, with this little hollow reed.

"You resist, my boy," said Bouscarle, "you resist and sink to the depths. Let yourself yield; make yourself limp. Let yourself live life without thinking that you're playing the flute, and then you will play."

He spoke the truth. Worn out from struggling, at that moment when all the stars sped through the sky like so much grain in the wind, I played. It rose from the heart in a sudden bound, gradually making me lighter. And through the barrel of my flute, I emptied myself, like a good fountain purges itself of its dark water.

OURS WAS a large farm; we had twenty thousand sheep. Five large sheepfolds lined the road to hold them all throughout the winter. At this time of poor grazing in the dry marshes, they would lick the salt at the base of the plants, and nibble the red behen. And knowing that there wasn't a flower to be found, the bees, who are the flies of the grass, made a leap of more than ten kilometers over our area.

On the day of the great departure, Bouscarle took the reins of the whole farm and began shaking the bit hard. Everyone's mouth bled, and I myself no longer mattered. Yet he was the one who had guided my fingers over the flute, who had put me, weak as I was, before the gaze of the sheep. But now he gave me no more notice than the hundred other shepherd's helpers who buzzed around the packed bags. The proprietor approached in a fine flowered waistcoat just at the moment when the animals began to pour out of the first door, which had been raised like a floodgate. There was snorting, galloping, climbing over hedges, and at the far end of the great fields, dogs from distant farms barked. Our boss went straight over to the proprietor. He was glowing black with anger, as fearful to the touch as hot tar. He said some words. I saw them. I didn't hear them in all that noise; I saw them in the white of his teeth, and the curl of his mustache, and in the disdainful spit that Bouscarle aimed right into the dust. I saw those words, and I also saw the proprietor go off, humbled, his tail between his legs, and the boss whose look was like a knife in his back, that's all I can say. Each to his own place.

ORDER returned, the foreman bellowing the long cries of the language of sheep the whole length of the sky, and that started the flow, thick and fast. And the road, taken by surprise, had already begun to groan and creak from every one of its stones, and great bands of magpie and hoopoe clattered around us like holiday streamers. A holiday, yes, the long-awaited holiday!

THEN, before taking his first step ahead of the animals, before taking command of that white road, the boss Bouscarle approached the saddle packs where I was tightening up the straps. He rested a heavy hand on my shoulder and I felt the sweat from it through my shirt. I turned my head and looked up at him; this was no longer the same man.

He glowed with the great rays of his sweat.

"My boy," he said, "don't think you know everything. You know the sheep, but to know is to be separate from. Now try to love; to love is to join. Then, you will be a shepherd."

Ah! How well I knew I was only a little apprentice. But among them, I was one of the best, and he had guided my fingers along the length of the flute. I knew well enough that I couldn't be quickly forgotten, even by the brain that drew forward twenty thousand sheep.

And yet, he did forget me; at least everything led me to believe that.

We moved out for long days across the breadth of a plain as red as raw flesh. I led a pack mule. That is, I just walked along beside him and tapped him on the nose when he sniffed out the shade of some cypress or stretched his mouth toward the nettle. The dust burned my eyes; blood red, it got into my mouth; it stuck to my tongue; deep in my throat, it was mud. I could never count on being able to see the one leading the other mule up ahead, a thousand sheep away, unless I took advantage of a sudden drop in the wind. It was no easier to see the one behind. And soon, the wind itself no longer reached us because the airborne earth that followed us was too thick. Lost, rolled along in the herd like a bit of gravel, I held myself together around this shepherd's love. I knew he was there, kilometers ahead, leading the way, marking the route. And from time to time, I felt along my thigh the fine roundness of the flute which clacked against the horn handle of my knife. I had a goatskin flask with a little more than a liter of fresh water in it; once in a while, I drank a little. The days stretched out; they extended over the earth. They had to be crossed from one end to the other by putting one foot ahead of the next. From time to time, the great phantom of a cypress appeared in the dust before me. It passed alongside, oblivious, following its own route, and I walked along mine. Sometimes, through the dust we saw a farm, pale and wide. Behind us, the whole country moaned with the moaning of the stragglers. At night, we stopped in little villages, all closed up like startled tortoises. Everything was dead. The one with the pack mule behind and the one with the pack mule ahead came up to me on aching feet. We remained there, listening to the great dust resettling.

The one from up front said, "The boss has passed Villeneuve-les-Orges. That's what a cart driver told me."

Or maybe:

"They told me that the boss is farther than Saint-Raphaël-des-Roches, in the Luberon valley."

And all at once, I despaired of this great land, of all this country that had to pass under our feet. When I slept, I dreamed of the ball of the earth, this great ball of the earth, and I had to straddle it with my legs wide apart like they do with wooden balls in the circus, and I was split in two up through my stomach and chest.

Sometimes, the one from behind said, "The *mas!* . . ."

He said no more, and he kept tasting these words on his lips, because he had left a lover behind there.

And so I thought of the *mas* as something lost in the depths of time, under layers and layers of rotting forests that had been dead for a hundred million turns of the earth.

Then we set off again, getting underway with no order. Or rather, on a silent order coming on the wings of the air. The sheep rose, the mules rose, we had to follow. And we began walking again over the wide earth in the roiling dust.

And so I went, thinking of nothing but the suffering of my flesh, until it brought me to tears, nothing but this great spine of fatigue running through me, until evening, when we made a twelve-hour-long stop in a village as cool and leafy as a peach on a tree. My two companions slept. As soon as the noise died down, and then its echo in the leaves of the high elms, I heard the song of the fountains. Water!

It was a beautiful fountain, flat-nosed as a bee. It spoke out of three mouths at once, three long stories of water full of watercress, of fish, eel, and frogs; it spoke of lovely footbaths and of a long open-mouthed drink.

I was leaving when a lamb leaned against my legs. It was covered with snot and couldn't open its muzzle, blind with mucous. Its head was only a block of mortar and it was looking for the spring by knocking its gourd of a skull along the coping.

So I took it in my arms, washed it, and gave it water to suck by filling my hand and making a teat with my thumb. Then I let it go, and it moved away toward its mother, water splattering in the sun.

And that night, I knew that it was not only the flute that the shepherd Bouscarle had shown me by guiding my fingers over the holes in the reed, but all of life:

"Don't think about playing, and then you will play . . ."

I looked at myself in the pool. I did not recognize my face. From a boy I had become a man; from a man I had become a shepherd. The radiance of my sweat dazzled me.

AT THAT point, the shepherd's voice changed as he offered me some dried figs.

"And then, I have six nice fresh *poivre d'âne* cheeses. If you'd like some."

WE TOOK up summer quarters in a high pasture in the vicinity of the Croix pass. The glaciers had taken this whole area in hand and raised it up to the sky. Great frozen fingers held grass. It was rich enough to make any healthy beast mad. The meadowsweet was as thick as cream and the soles of our espadrilles turned green from its juice just from walking in the pasture.

I spent long days lying on my back, sucking on my flute, from time to time pushing out some little curling note. My blood grew calm. But I stored up my experience, and more and more, especially in the evening hours, I thought of the words of Bouscarle and I heard the step of the great gods.

I drank from the sky in long mouthfuls, like water from the pool of that fountain where I'd seen the first rays of the shepherd reflected back at me.

The sheep were spread throughout the valley and on its slopes. They reached right to the edges of a village as lean as a pauper.

I am going to tell you the secret.

The shepherd's true occupation, only one thing teaches that: the sky. For a long time after that in my life, I weighed them, weighed them in my hands, and passed them from one hand to the other, all those words of Bouscarle. And I understood that those words meant two things: one thing that you understood immediately, another thing that you understood slowly, gradually over time.

"This Jesus is not the great vastness, but that little bit of night, over there, with one star, just one." Say that to a fifteen-year-old peasant coming out of church after singing by the crèche. He looks at the star; he looks at the finger pointing to the star. He says yes; he hasn't understood.

He hasn't completely understood.

But, when it's a man of my age who has chewed this over through the years, all alone, each time adding a bit of his own human experience to his reflection, then there is some chance for the second meaning to light up like a lamp.

One star, one alone. And now, look at the night completely flooded with stars!

There are the powers of the world. That is the secret!

This is what he meant:

"Son, you have heard our pastor. He's told you a beautiful story of the little child who was not received by the hands of midwives, but by the straw, as the beasts are received. He told you that it was a virgin who made him. The beasts are virgins; they do not soil the acts that make life. They make life, simple as that. They go into the bushes, and then they come out with baby sheep and, right away, these babies taste fresh life with their muzzles, and right away, they are heavy with a great wisdom which astonishes men. The crèche, the straw, the cattle, the donkey, the virgin, this birth: among men, this is the birth of a healthy animal. That is the great lesson. That is why men crucified the child."

To know all that would have helped me, but I didn't know it then, and I played the flute.

But this flute playing, it wasn't by accident that Bouscarle had put the reed to my lips. In this flute was all the knowledge of the sky. It was the reed that's planted in the bank's porous flesh to make fountains spring forth. I planted the flute in the sky. I took the other end in my mouth. And the music was only the noise I made filling myself with sky.

When we reached the mountain, Bouscarle named the seconds-in-command. Ours was a meat-eater from Pontet, a knowledgeable man, nearly as knowledgeable as Bouscarle, except for the simple difference that he didn't know the great words to make the herds start off, and that came from his liking meat nearly raw and being too saturated with blood.

One evening he came over to me, his eyebrows knitted together with worry. He studied the sheep in a peculiar way.

"Son," he said to me, "go over to Corne-Blanche. You'll find Bouscarle there. Ask him this for me: 'Have you gotten wind of the planet?' No more. Then, come back and tell me his answer."

Instead of being scattered all over the grass, our herd was clotted together in big lumps of trembling beasts.

I went, and when it was late, I saw the boss' lantern. He was sitting next to it. The boys of the "Vermeil" pasture were also there, and those who kept watch in the pastures of Norante, all of them, maybe thirty, bent over their staffs, all ears turned toward Bouscarle who breathed not a word.

I was about to speak when someone said to me, "Yes, we know."

"And so?" I said.

"And so! . . ."

And someone next to Bouscarle shook his head, his forehead low and silent. And I leaned on my stick, too, and I waited like the others.

"Who has hit the beasts?" asked Bouscarle gently.

Someone answered, "Me!"

"Come here."

It was a heavy-set man from Arles, dark and gray as a cicada.

"I mean," Bouscarle continued, looking at the man, "did you hit them without just cause?"

The Arlatan said nothing for a moment, and then, "Yes, I hit them without just cause."

"Then," said Bouscarle, "go down to the village while there's still time, and stay there."

"It's as bad as that," breathed a shepherd next to me. Then he raised his hand to be noticed, and said, "Me, too, I hit them, boss."

"No, you should have said that a moment ago. I need everyone. I want to save what can be saved, but I need men. If it's true, if you have hit them, take your chances; too bad for you, I'm keeping you here."

Then he asked, "And the dogs—"

And then, along the embankment of the path where they could be seen as though it were broad daylight because of the moon's reflection on the glaciers, we noticed the dogs running with their heads down toward the valleys.

I returned to my boss to tell him all this and I thought of that shepherd's "It's as bad as that," and it seemed to me that somehow we must have gotten ourselves into deep trouble of some very strange kind.

I told the shepherd from Pontet what I thought.

He pointed to the sky, but I didn't see anything.

"Remember when the sun set yesterday."

I tried to remember. Nothing.

"You didn't smell the sulfur?"

"No!"

Then I remembered that the day before I had played my flute just as the sun went down. And I picked up my flute and sniffed the holes. And then, yes, I smelled the sulfur.

"It's the planet," he said.

DAWN ARRIVED like any other. No different, except for our flock, still all clotted together like bad milk, and our dog, who could not stop trembling and wouldn't leave my side. I went to my boss' hut.

"Macimin!" I cried.

But the hut was empty. He had grabbed his blankets, shoulder bag, staff, and flask, and he had taken off. A shiver ran up my spine especially as the dog came to sniff the empty hut, looked up at me, looked at the sheep, and then took two little steps across the grass. The sheep were asleep. The dog took off, extending himself into a long gallop. Then, the sheep stood up. It was understood; they had risen and they hadn't shaken their heads like sheep just waking up, but instead they tilted their ears to catch the whistling of the grass under the galloping feet of the dog, to trace his route. The dog stopped in his tracks; he sniffed the wind; he tried to lie low, to make his way back toward me along the lower, hidden trail. Then a huge mass of sheep, packed together belly-to-belly, rolled forward to block his path.

I took my staff and started to run, crying, "Fédo! Fédo!" when I heard Bouscarle's voice in my ear, "If you have hit them, too bad for you."

And I stayed on my hillock to watch.

All the clots of sheep were on the move like clouds in the grass. They ran, making great circles, following a plan they cried out to one another in an entirely new kind of bleat. The panic-stricken dog was dancing about in the thick of them. Finally, they surrounded him, and he knew that his last moment had arrived. He no longer put up a fight, but I saw the sheep close in on him, engulf him, trample him, trample him to death, with the great mindfulness required of a thing that has to be done well.

I ran toward the rocks. From there, you could look down over our whole region and then the "Vermeil" meadow and a bit of Norante. Above, I found the boss stretched out on the ground, his hat over his eyes, and fourteen of our poor men, their lips white with fear.

Because, below, it was like a thunderstorm had struck. A stampede of running sheep filled the valleys. It tore up the fences. It seethed in beasts who leaped against our rocky hill. It ripped up the earth, and it ran in torrents as determined as rushing water. In the midst of this noise, we heard the village below sound its alarm. When night came, the boss lifted his hat. He said to us, "Count the fires."

We focused our eyes to count the watch fires. There were no longer any more of ours. Far off, on the mountain's large back, there were the other herds from Arles, Crau, Camargue, Albaron. And someone said, "Master, there are the five Crau fires, the three Albaron fires, and ten for the Camargue."

"Watch them carefully," the boss told him.

He stared wide-eyed until it hurt. He stayed there a good minute, and then he cried, "Master, master, they're going out, they're going out, no more Albaron fires, no more fires for the Crau, no more for the Camargue. Nothing's left, master, nothing, they've all gone out."

The boss lay down again, and covered his eyes with his hat. As though he were speaking to himself, we heard him say, "Over there, too. So, it's the great revolt."

So THAT was what I saw, me, a little shepherd, something seen only once in a hundred years, this revolt of the beasts, on an order that came from the sky, with the smell of sulfur. This was what I saw, and this was what I did.

I took up my flute, and I played very softly, for myself, I played this fear in my heart and the great voice of the mystery. That night, throughout the world, there was a terrible noise of sheep bleating and of bells from the church towers, of wooden houses cracking, and the cries of men, and the cries of women, and a great angry stream which hurtled down the steps of the mountains.

Bouscarle said, "Play for us all."

Then, I took a good mouthful of air, and with all the fullness of my breath, I began to play the flute for us all.

· .

IT WAS getting late. Only a little meadow of sun remained up high on the hill between the evening overflowing into the valleys and the sky gleaming like new iron. We climbed toward Césaire's. He was there in front of his clearing, his arms dangling at his sides, his hands heavy with clay. The kiln was smoking.

In a little grass nest, the shepherd carried his sheep milk cheeses tucked in his arm.

"I saw the sheep pass by," said Césaire, between mouthfuls. "They made the day tremble. They poured over the whole road."

I spoke, too, of the herds from that morning, that great flood of animals running through the straits of Mirabeau and their stop near the fountain.

The shepherd listened. Then he asked for the postal calendar. He looked at the card, pointing to the days with his finger. Then he said, "This is the day, or rather, the night, this is the night. Césaire, we ought to leave."

Césaire looked at the pale woman, the red-haired girl and the children, then me.

"And him?" he said.

"Him? We'll take him along."

I believed we were leaving for a gathering of the shepherds. The haste with which everything had been decided, the slow advice of the white woman, "Take your coat, take along the blanket, let him have grandfather's coat," left me a little nervous in the end. Then the shepherd looked at the county map on the other side of the calendar and I saw his finger trace far into the white of the back country.

Then Césaire said, "We'll have to borrow Chabrillan's horse, and so we'll have to leave right away because if we don't, the farm gates will be closed and we'll lose more time when there's none to spare."

Then I asked softly, "Are we going far?"

"We're going there!" said the shepherd.

I looked at where his finger pointed. It was the Mallefougasse plateau.

I only knew of the Mallefougasse because I had heard talk of it. All the stallholders I had kept company with before finding shelter under the thick, leafy branches of Césaire and the shepherd had spoken to me of that country at one time or another. Each time, it was the end of the world. But I especially remember Pierrinet the horse dealer, when he placed his hand sideways, half on the café table, half off it, and what he said to me, "Mallefougasse is like that. It's still a little bit attached to the earth. Although. . . ! But, above, below, it's all sky. It's like something stuck out into the sky. The sky is all around that land like a sucking mouth. Do you understand?"

I had understood then. I understood much better now. I understood that finger resting on the flimsy calendar map, Césaire who was borrowing a horse, and everything that was going to carry me, rolled in the grandfather's coat, toward that land the sky sucked like a mouth.

At the Chabrillans', the gates were closed.

"I knew it," said Césaire, "when you're in a hurry, it's always like that."

We banged on the gate with our fists and our feet; that set the iron chains clanging. We cried out, "Bartholomé! Bartholomé! Of all the luck! Are you going to wake up or not?"

The farm went on sleeping, eyes shut tight. But the dogs howled in the yard.

"All the same, we're making a hell of a noise," said the shepherd. "What if they aren't there?"

"That can't be it," said Césaire, "there'd have to be some disaster. They have a little girl. They wouldn't have left her alone."

He bellowed once more, "Bartholomé!" and then he added hoarsely, "Christ, I've done in my vocal chords!"

But this time, a little line of light shone around a closed shutter. The shutter began to open.

"Who's there?" demanded a woman's voice.

"Ah!" cried Césaire, relieved. "Is that you, Anaïs? What a lot of sleep for such a little woman! Wake up Bartholomé."

"Who are you?"

"Ah, Anaïs, come on, unplug your ears. It's Césaire from the pottery. You know who it is, Bartholomé!"

"He isn't here."

"Where is he?"

"He went to the village!"

"He's crazy!"

"No, he needed to see Pancrace, and Pancrace is only there in the evening, so he had to stay."

"We want you to lend us Bijou," said Césaire, "and the cart. The three of us have to go that way, and it's alright with your Bartholomé."

Anaïs remained silent for a moment, and then she said, "I don't open the gate. I'm afraid at night, I don't open it. Wait for Bartholomé."

"But we don't have time, Anaïs. Are you crazy or what? You know very well that it's me. You can hear me talking. What, you don't recognize the way I talk? For goodness sake, it's me! Once more, it's me,

Césaire, and Barberousse the shepherd, and someone from town, a friend. Come on, open up, cheese head!"

She remained, up against her idea there in her window. She leaned with her bare arms on the bar and she answered everything Césaire said with her "yes, but . . . ," "yes, but. . . ."

"Yes, but, you know, there are times . . . it's like this, it seems like a voice but it isn't, . . . times at night, it's the work of the devil. It seems like Césaire, and then you open up, and then. . . ."

And Césaire was completely out of patience, pacing in circles like a mule on the threshing ground, and Barberousse was swearing into his beard, when Bartholomé arrived, carrying a lantern. The lamp gave him a shadow a kilometer long.

"Ah!" he said, "yes." Then, yes again, but he didn't have the time to get his bearings. Césaire pushed him through the gate, and from there to the stable, and soon Bijou, all harnessed, arrived.

"Close it, close it!" cried Césaire. "We only have time to leave."

Already two rises of land were rolling us into the great wave of hills, far from the gates where Bartholomé stood, lantern raised.

IT MIGHT have been eleven o'clock at night judging from the Reillanne church tower bells, but it was hard to tell because of the wind and especially because of the swinging wagon, creaking and groaning in the hard waves of the earth.

Then we entered the great Sans-Bois wilderness and the stars leaned down right to its slatted sides.

"It will take us three hours," said the shepherd.

Our pilot was Césaire. He looked at the sky to find the path. The stars, it seemed, marked it.

"You see," he said, "we are going to pass between that one and that one."

Then he pulled on the bit a few times to wake up Bijou who was fast asleep.

We went down into the depths of the earth, as if into whirlpools. We heard jaws closing over the emptiness of our wake, or we rose again to the fragile and trembling summit of a hill in all the muted noise of the stars.

At other times, a wide flat stretch carried us along without dip or rise; coasting smoothly, we glided over a plateau. Bijou's big hoofs lapped the sand. Then it seemed to us that over there, in front of us, other vessels sped along. Then we saw they were immobile, as if anchored. The pilot pulled on the leather helm and we skimmed past huge rustling chestnut trees like reefs. The night frothed under such flights and frolics, and the heavy swimming of boars ripped apart the juniper bushes. On our vessel, there were three of us. Césaire, who was looking for the path of stars, and Barberousse, who didn't say a word, and me. Ever since I had felt the heaving breath of the earth under the boat, I was as lost as a kitten and I hung for dear life onto Césaire's velour jacket.

We reached the great slope. Barberousse let out a cry. Césaire used all his strength to come to a stop. All three of us stood up on the trembling boards of the cart.

As far as the eye could see, the plateau descended toward the distant chasm of the Durance. There were so many stars overhead that in the gray light, you could make out the short spray of the heather and lavender, and below, very far away and very much lower, the scaly skin of the Durance.

"Too late," cried Barberousse.

He pointed out to us, off in the distance, four large squat fires which were no longer anything but coals. The whole great slope of the plateau flowed with herds. You didn't see them, you heard the noise of their cascade, and the shepherds' whistles, and the swaying of the lanterns that they rocked slowly in the night to give the sheep a rhythm to walk by. The alpine roads already sounded like streams. Too late! The shepherds were leaving.

Ahead of us, a great land had just been swallowed up as if by the sea.

III

In the preceding pages, you will have found an obsession with water and the sea. That's because a herd is a liquid thing, a marine thing.

From Crau to the Alpe, there are only dry rivers, streams which transport cicadas and lizards. The herds climb into the thorns and the furnaces of dust. Yes, but this flood grating the ground with its belly, this wool, this deep, monotonous noise, it all gives the shepherds souls that possess the resonant movement and weight of the sea.

Summer days on the mountain plateaus, the shepherd stretches out in the grass with his face to the sky. The clouds have a life of seaweed and algae, blooming grasses in the breasts of the wave like fountains of milk in the breasts of women. Sometimes, when the expanse is all blue, after the north wind passes, a little white sail still makes its way in the high winds toward the horizon's distant ports.

Finally, this love shepherds have for water and the sea, this obsession which, up there, on the high ground, makes them speak of pilots, helms, sails, waves, sand, spray, flight, swimming, gulfs, and depths, this great affinity is traced deep in their flesh. Because the occupation of the masters of beasts is something like water which runs through the fingers and which cannot be held. Because that odor of suint and wool, that odor of man cooked in his own sweat, that odor of ram and goat, that odor of milk and of full ewes, that odor of nascent lambs rolled in their slime, that odor of dead beasts, that odor of herds in the high mountain summer pastures, that is life, like the brine of the great seas.

RETURNING toward Saint-Martin-l'Eau, we saw rising out of the beauty of the sunrise the perched village of Dauphin. Césaire let us wait for him by the bridge and he took the shortcut to lead Bijou back to his stable. The shepherd went into the Largue up to his knees. He bent over the water, watching the slow life below. With his hand, he fished out a barbel round as an eggplant, and then he drew from a hole a long angry eel that flipped around his arm. Césaire came back from above with fist-fuls of green peppers. At that moment, the sky was milky and the day promised to be beautiful. As we arrived at the pottery, the young sorceress arrived, too, skin and bones, covered with dust, dust packed hard on her thin legs by a long night of running. Then I understood that she had run behind our cart. We skinned the still-live eel, and the skin billowed in the wind. We put the barbel on an iron grill and, over a fire of vine shoots, it all began to cook; the eel in a fennel stock, the fish on the grill. The girl carefully basted the fish with oil.

The shepherd worked a bit. He learned with a sigh that the ewe Joséphine had given birth and he went to wipe off the lamb with swabs of grass. Then he brought it to us, still all trembling, all sticky, all surprised. The smell of newborn lamb mixed with the smell of our soup, our fire, and then came the smell of the dawn, that scent of awakened earth and trees coming back to life. The sky began to moan again softly under the sun.

We blamed all we had missed the night before on that fear-ridden Anaïs. It was that great drama of the earth that the masters of beasts put on every year, the night of the summer solstice.

· ·

I RETURNED to Manosque by the most convenient route. The walking, my strength, the eel soup had given me heart and I rolled along the paths like a stone, but I was hungry for that great thing of the spirit and I couldn't think of anything else. Insensible to the beautiful flower of sky, to all the hoopoes that were learning to fly around me, I went along and my thoughts, like a fledgling bird, learned to fly, too. They took off in the direction of that odor of newborn lamb.

"No more rest!" I had written to Césaire. This is what I said to him:

"This is what you must do, watch carefully for the date and the time for me. Try to find out, let me know exactly. Twenty opinions are better than one. Then, I put you in charge of the whole business because, you know, I am so far away from it all, I am so far from it, because, when all is said and done, I haven't been able to completely disengage myself from the easy life, because I have a family that is used to it, because Manosque isn't a big town, but it's a town all the same. Do you know what I mean? I'm telling you this so that you will know that I'm putting the whole business in your hands. I know that I myself could never learn the time and date. I would have to go spend days and days in the hills and it would be exactly the moment I close my eyes when that red scarf would pass, and once more I would miss everything. Watch well and then tell me when it is close to the time. I'll arrange to be ready day or night. Send me a message, and I'll come up at once. Warn Anaïs and Bartholomé and, if perhaps you could get a faster horse. . . . Ah yes, Césaire, if only my life were like yours. To hollow out a burrow and to live there with only those you love for company. Maybe I would have had a witch daughter, too. Now, it's too late. A hug for everyone there."

And I added to my letter a word to Barberousse. It was in a visiting card envelope and on the bottom I wrote, "For the shepherd." I said to him, "Barberousse, so here's how it stands. We must not miss the shepherds' thing again. You talked to me about sheep, and the revolt, and your master who is buried in Saint-Martin-de-Crau. That filled me with longing. I have written to Césaire for him to watch for the man with the red scarf. Césaire, as you know, is a good man, but he has his work. He can't spend all his time watching the road. I need to be sure; that's why I'm writing to you, too. You, you get wind of things in the air. You said to me (you'll remember), 'The eagle's shadow wakes you' and then, 'there, it's the same thing.' I want to ask you for a favor. Watch for me. I need to be there when the shepherds do their play. I'll tell you why. It's because I want to copy down what they say on paper, and then afterwards show it to people to make them see that shepherds aren't just shepherds, but, as you say, the masters of the beasts. My warmest greetings."

Those letters calmed my anxiousness for three days. Then, Lardeyret who drives a stage cart between Manosque and Simiane came to bring me the response. It was, "Good, count on it" on Césaire's part and, on the part of Barberousse, "That's fine."

I would have liked something more definite.

I would wake in the middle of the night. It seemed to me that the days had run from everywhere like water through a basket. The calendar was downstairs in the kitchen. To go down, to check it, was to make noise on the steps, knock over chairs, upset the whole house. I remained sitting up in bed. Let's see, yesterday, Thursday. It's February; the wind is in the chimney, the bare branch of the rosebush scratching the window. Until June 24th, there was time. February! The sheep were in their shelters, in Crau, and the shepherds were playing lotto in the cafés in Arles and Salon. Sleep, you have time.

Other times, in the thick of night, nothing indicated the season. Memories of past Junes were there alive all around me, the noise of watering in the fields, the smell of sap rising in the fig trees, the big leaves and the wind. All that so faint; I stopped breathing. The silence deceived my ears with its eternal drone.

I wrote another letter to Césaire, another note to Barberousse.

"Watch out," I said, "It'll soon be time. It's May, I've already seen some of them."

And Lardeyret came back with the answers:

"Don't worry."

One morning, I tore off the page for May 31st from the calendar. There underneath was the month of June, as well hidden as a green lizard.

The first day didn't budge. The second day, a little uneasiness drifted in a long wind under a brand new sky, but the third day the tide of sheep overflowed from the hills to the south and the western passes at the same time, and the great froth-browed herds made their way into our country.

At last, a telegram was delivered to me, opened, all torn and crumpled, read by at least the hundred or so Jeans of Manosque. It was simply addressed to Monsieur Jean. It said, "Forward!" and it was signed Césaire.

"Yes," I said to the carrier, "yes, it's for me, don't worry, I know what it is."

"Sure?"

"Sure!"

And I took my good curved walking stick. The sky played ball with that great noise of herds and all the echoes from the hills trembled with bleating.

They had taken care of everything. Barberousse waited for me above Saint-Magloire in the open oaks. He had brought his long willow wood horn, and he sounded a good long and well-blown note in the direction of the pottery.

He explained to me, "First, it's to tell him, 'be ready,' and then it's to tell him, 'relax, he's here.' What worries we've had!"

And, in the clearing, the wagon was all ready and on the point of setting out to sea. Césaire was up on the seat and holding onto a little black-and-white mare with both fists, her back end dancing around and splashing the prow of the cart with her long tail shivering like rippling water. She clattered her four hooves impatiently.

We quickly settled in. Barberousse went to the back, on the blankets. I had the grandfather's coat again. I was next to the pilot, and this time we took with us the young sorceress with the yellow eyes.

The departure was so sudden that all four of us let out an "Oh!" This cry sounded shrilly in the mare's ear and she shot off at full speed like a fish, and already the foam from the grass spurted out along beside us.

This first swim into the hill's surf I will remember all my life. All along that wild slope descending toward Saint-Michel and over which Césaire led us by shortcuts, our wagon, its sides too high, swayed right and left through the waves of thyme. We hung on to the stays.

Sometimes, a "Watch your heads!" from Césaire made us crouch down into the hold, and we passed full speed through the foam of a chestnut tree, through the lower branches.

Sometimes in the middle of flat country, a bit reassured by our wake stretched out like a thread, a high wave lifted us up to make us touch the sky. We fell back down, all askew, every joint creaking, and I said to myself, "In case of shipwreck, you jump onto the tiller and you stay there!"

Finally, the two wheels landed level on the hard road. Césaire stopped the mare, wiped his forehead, took up the reins again, and asked, "What time is it?"

Oh! This time we were rich in navigational instruments.

Barberousse rummaged around in his jacket and drew out his big watch.

"Eight o'clock," he said.

"We're okay," said Césaire. And then, "*Avanti!*"

And with a loop of the reins, he stung the mare's rear.

NIGHT came.

We sliced through the village of Ongles at a trot-gallop, extended and solid. The milestone at the turn sparked under our iron wheels. People came out of the café to look at our cloud of dust. From there, we skirted around a horn of Lure, into a little valley which raised its high wave of bare rocks in warning. At Saint-Etienne, we stopped under the plane trees to light our lantern. It was just a bottle with a hole in the bottom and a candle stuck inside it. Barberousse held it out above us.

We followed along Lure, but by a snaking route that wove round all the contours of the high hill like twines of ivy. The breath of the high ground cut across us with sudden gusts of wind as cold and solid as blocks of ice. Barberousse used his whole body to protect the candle, and then he extended a wing of his greatcoat, and we heard the sail clap and the mare galloped. My belly was all tickly from the rises. The swell of the open sea carried us along as its waves of earth unrolled.

A detour faced us into the wind at the mouth of a valley. The candle went out. The mare, who'd gotten a blast of wind right in her nostrils, stopped dead against the darkness. Césaire tacked gently into the night. I hung onto the sides.

"Prepare the matches."

The wind whipped us on the sides, two turns of the wheels, and then it hit us right on the back.

"Light them."

And we had to face the stampede once again.

We had gone past Cruis.

"What time is it?" asked Césaire.

"Hold the candle, my girl."

Barberousse fished around and found his watch. We had not stopped galloping.

"A little after nine."

"Good. *Avanti!*"

"Give me the candle, my girl."

One last hill threw us right into the open sky.

"Oh!" cried Césaire and Barberousse.

"Oh!" I cried.

"Oh!" said the girl softly against my ear.

The mare, held hard, reared up like struck water. We had arrived!

As far as you could see, the heavy sea of herds was lapping the black earth. It began there, under the mare's feet, and it extended over the whole of Mallefougasse. Despite the darkness, you could see it. All the stars had descended upon the earth; they were the eyes of the sheep lit up by the watchfires, by the four bonfires, by all the Saint-Jean fires that illuminated the countryside from here to the distant mountains of the Mées, and of Peyruis, Saint-Auban, and Digne. You could hear the last shepherds to arrive whistling and the bells of the rams and the mules, and far off in the distance, toward Sisteron, the clusters of dogs howling, necks extended, into the moonless night. . . .

"Pause! Pause! Pause!" sang the shepherds to the sheep.

Men ran by, hands raised toward the new herds. The animals lay down in a mass around them. You could hear them kneeling down on the ground, crushing the hyssop. The whole heavy batter of herds turned slowly like a whirlpool of mud.

"Fédo, Fédo," sang the shepherds, to reassure the ewes.

On the crest of the hill, someone tried the aeolian harps, then tightened the keys. A cord broke and the moan traveled on the wind to the depths of the county, toward the Durance lowlands. Men's voices called for strings. The tympon players played their bright scales, and then blew the warning notes, and a shiver of fear like wind on the sea raised the waves of beasts again. Young shepherds carried tubs of water. One of them, with the lantern, walked backwards, lighting the way. A little lost harmonica sounded in a juniper.

"Téou, Téou, Téou!" said the shepherds to calm the beasts.

Everything fell silent.

That "téou," the word of peace, sang itself through the whole expanse. Afterwards, there was silence, and then the voice of a few masters, and then the great silence.

Someone tried the music conductor's whistle. The aeolian harps murmured. Someone whistled. Silence.

Césaire had tied up the mare. As an extra precaution, he had hobbled her legs with a blanket.

"On a night like this, you never know."

We walked toward the clearing.

The shepherds were sitting all around. Despite the two hundred men and the hundred thousand beasts, there was so little noise that you could hear us coming. Heads turned toward us; someone made room. I squatted down in the folds of my coat. My arms shook. I took out my notebook and pencils. Barberousse gave me a board to write on.

Four huge fires lit up and defined the large stage of grass and earth.

Right in the middle, a man was standing. He was waiting for what would flow from his heart. I remember that he was a tall, thin man, one who saw things, who feasted on visions. His nose turned into a bird's beak under the fire's high flames. He was wearing a red scarf on his head, tied gypsy-fashion.

Suddenly he raised his hand to greet the night. A rumbling flowed from the aeolian harps. The muffled flutes sang like springs.

"The worlds," said the man, "were in the god's net like tuna in the madrague..."

You could have heard him on the other sides of the earth and the sky.

IV

I've been asked many times—every time I relate this shepherds' play—if this ceremony was part of some esoteric tradition. I don't know. I don't believe that it was a ceremony. I'm the one who says "shepherds' *plays;*" they say, "We're going to perform." All the same, there are arguments for and against. To find out the truth, you would have to go stay with them through the long months in the high summer pastures, get on familiar terms with them, share their breadcrusts rubbed with garlic, and take part in those long tales of summer nights. If all goes well, by next year, I'll have untangled the mystery. I now have a friend among the true masters of the beasts. It's Vénérande, the head shepherd from the Saint-Trubat farm, and it's agreed that next season, I'll go up to spend the long months with him.

So, for me, and for the moment, I believe that it's simply a game, a pastime, but the pastime of the masters of beasts. All the rest, everything that Barberousse could say about it, who's getting old, who's a dreamer, and who, I know, is capable of falling under the simple spell of a fountain, all the rest lies under the shadow of clouds. There is, of course, the Sardinian . . .

But, as for the Sardinian, let me explain. The Sardinian—that thin man in the red scarf from whom the whole game spatters like water shaken from a dog—the Sardinian, he's the author. He's the midwife of images. Moreover, he is, I know, a remarkable midwife for difficult ewes. He has long and nervous hands, as delicate as little fish, and if you had to give him all the lambs he brought to life in the furrow of his two hands, he would be richer than the richest proprietors. For the images, for the plays, it's the same. They are all there around him, pregnant and heavy with dreams, with the beautiful coil of the serpent of stars, and, in the midst of them, he's the midwife of the play. He's the one who delivers the play and who makes sure it's born completely new each time, because each time, it is born completely new, and year after year, the same words are never repeated, nor the same roles, and each time, the play has that odor of the blood and salt of newborn lambs, because everyone makes it up. The Sardinian, who is the narrator, may keep a narrative thread in his hand, always the same, that's possible, but those around him, those shepherds who are like a seated shadow and whom you don't see until the moment they move forward between the fires, those shepherds are never the same. Maybe you would say what Barberousse said to me.

"That one, it's five years now that he's been playing. That one, I've seen him twice. Those over there are new, but they help the Glaude master, and he speaks so well that he must have taught them their parts."

No, Barberousse, the same shepherd never sits at the edge of the play twice. You tell me, "It's five years for that one," yes, but he's five years older, five years richer. In that time, he has experienced things on the world's wide back, he isn't the same. He won't say what he said five years ago, or what he said last year, but all that he's learned in this new year. You know, Barberousse, dreams are the shepherd's savings. And, very soon, he will spend this year's savings like a boy on holiday.

Do you want me to tell you?

One fine day—one fine night, rather—the Sardinian will come again to raise his hand in greeting, and then maybe in the shadow's wide circle there will be a young shepherd, yes, Barberousse, a young shepherd, full to bursting. And when someone calls, "the Sea," or "the River" or "the Woods," it'll be that young shepherd who comes forward to speak. And you will all listen, because you are masters and you know what is beautiful. Because you are masters of the beasts and you know first of all how to be masters of yourselves when your self-love or your spitefulness want to take over. And the young shepherd will speak so well that he will become the future master. The Sardinian will give him the red woolen scarf and the great herd of your dreams will flow behind him, toward other pastures.

HOWEVER, seeing this Mallefougasse plateau, these black lands clawed by the rain, these rocks that a sand plane has worn to flat tables, these trees in their homespun cloaks turning their backs on the sky's anger, this solitude, this great voice, the spirit is immediately seized with the noble sadness and the memory of high places.

The grass is of a green gold and, when the wind ruffles it, it discovers its age underneath, as old as the earth. Blue schist, completely bare, creaks under the sun in fits and starts and suddenly cascades down to the road, making all the echoes ring. Then everything falls still. The torrent of stone stops. The schist creaks. Mallefougasse lives a life which is not vegetable. The trees there have learned to keep quiet. It freely lives the life of earth and stones. Under that light curtain of flesh, blue rocks, clay-pits, quivering eyelids of sand, throbs the interior of the world.

Everything here is religion. There, in the crushed grass, is the litter of the gods!

The little village is made up of four houses lying level with the ground and a barn called "the lookout" because it raises the sly vent of its pulley window over a bank. The other walls are flat and windowless. The stones, unplastered, are eaten away by the wind. The doors have thick bolts, all glistening with oil, which slip into their cylinders like fat black rats, silent and solid. The people from here have that long unwavering look that goes to the core of things, through men, women, the hills, and the depths of the sky.

Thus, everything is ready on this high overhang of the earth to serve as altar and sacrificial stone, and yet, the shepherds have chosen it for other, more simple reasons.

In Crau, of course, the sheep have plenty of room, and then, there they are, in the worst of the heat along the narrow roads, squeezed together, running as one thick body, like water, with no air around them.

And so, they move through the areas where land is valuable, where, on plots the size of postage stamps, you can make money growing leeks, parsley, peaches, apricots, grapes. Just try letting them spread out there! You'll find a shotgun exploding in your ear. Thus, you go along your flat way from one dust cloud to another, without ever stepping beyond the telegraph poles, with only one desire nevertheless, to reach the land, yes, the land! The land of leeks, parsley, peach trees, that isn't land anymore. It's so mixed with night soil, manure, droppings, and dung that it has become human rottenness, and they can have it! No, the land, the great land, our own, the land that remained after the flood, has dried itself off and there it is, the land where there's room for everyone.

And Mallefougasse is it!

What's more, when you're there, you're at a point where you've come more than a hundred kilometers along the way, and you have more than a hundred kilometers left to go. So you have the right to rest. Nothing screams in you if you lie down by the side of the road. It's a stopping point, and it suits us just right. It's like a great pool. The water of herds fills it at leisure, laps a bit, and then sleeps. But what is most beautiful is the great breadth of it. You don't have to pay attention to this earth like a bit of the night, to the fearful trees, to the free movements of the wind, no, the sheep are at ease. They are there in the open, bathing in the air on all sides. The animals' sweat smokes as if someone had just set fire to the hill. The bees who have been prisoners in their wool since the Châteauneuf hives set themselves free, flying awkwardly in this too pure air and falling into the fleece of thyme and wormwood. The ewes give birth. The males go off to push their snouts straight into the north wind, filling their brains with the fresh air until they shake off the surplus with a sneeze that leaves them trembling with drunkenness. All the bad folk are far off.

Here, everything is new, land and men. You have wine from Arnoulas and water in seven lovely springs. Springs as round-faced as girls, all gushing and plump. It's true that this water is not welcoming and that it wells up without bindweed, without rushes, without periwinkle, without moss, from between bare lips of rock. But so what, must you always have frills? Can't you love cold water for being cold water and do you think you quibble over such things when you've just spent twenty days going through the dust rising from all of Provence? The water is all by itself in a stream of blue schist. It is the blue of the blue of cornflowers. When it lets out one of its braids, its white heart glistens. That's why we choose to stop at Mallefougasse. We don't have the same spans for measuring fear. For us, the country is wide, comfortable, flat. We have wine from Arnoulas and water in the little valley of seven springs, peace, the joy of feet. That's why!

And then, too, it's a kind of reunion. Sometimes you have things to say that you've saved for a whole year. You think, "I'll tell him that at Mallefougasse."

And so, it must have evolved quite naturally.

There, reunited on the sparseness of Mallefougasse, exhausted herds, heavy shepherds. Night came. They lit a fire. There was only the night full of stars, this land all alone under the sky, bordered all around by sky, and, as in the earliest times, an ocean of beasts surrounded a few men. They huddled close to the fire. The Sardinian was there that time. And he told stories about the stars above, about the earth below. He told them to make the night pass, and also because his heart was all reflections in which the soul of the world moved.

The next time, someone said to him, "Sardinian, stand up." He stood up, and now there were a few more shepherds because it had been repeated from pasture to pasture with "That Sardinian, really, if you could have heard him!"

The next time, word passed all around, "What if we perform? The

Sardinian would lead, and we would speak when it was our turn, what do you say, Sardinian?" And that's what they did and it went very well because, among the shepherds, the soul of the universe is like a ray of sunlight in water.

The next time, or maybe that time, the flute warbled in joy, in tune with the words.

And so, beginning from that moment, the infant-poem could walk sturdily. It was alive and well.

. .

THE STAGE, as I've said, is a square clearing of about twenty paces. At each corner is a fire which dances on pine and cedar boughs, heaps of dry thyme. Four shepherds are in charge of supplying the wood and herbs and, sometimes, when the flame dies down, they fan the coals briskly with leafy branches. These are actors that really count! First of all, it's from them that the light comes and it's from them that the scent comes, that essence of resin and burnt juniper that thickens the air and drifts off towards Ganagobie and makes the villages in the woods nervous.

The drama is accompanied by music, music for three instruments. I won't talk about that first instrument from which everything springs, from which all music has run, the freely singing earth which is there all around with its weight of animals, herds, trees, grass, wind, springs, the Durance rumbling deep in the valley. The others are the aeolian harp, the tympon, and the water jug. I've said how the aeolian harps are made, how the man merges with them to play them, or more precisely, to play the trees and the wind. But, the mixture of that human touch and that breath, master of time and racer through space, creates a god's voice which goes all the way to the harmonious depths of the horror.

It is a shepherd's invention. One of those secret and solitary harps unleashed fear throughout the whole region of Queyras, in '12 or '13, a little before the war. This was a village of simple people, with goiters heavy as melons, and for that reason, with heads bent toward the earth. This country has no water. The village is built on rock, hollowed by three long, dark and rumbling underground wells. The opening of the wells, capped by a hood of stone, remains locked with large key all day. The gate is only opened in the evening, just time for the women to draw buckets, to fill pails, to redden their hands on the rust from the chains, to wet their feet in the cool water, to laugh. . . . That particular shepherd, they say, wanted to drink and couldn't. He was told it was too late. He argued. Arguments with men with goiters always end in yelling and stone throwing. Our shepherd climbed back up his hill to his pasture and there, he made his harp. He claimed, afterwards, to have made it to distract himself, having, of course, forgotten the star branded on his forehead by a piece of flint. What's certain is that if this harp was made by chance, chance is a great master, because it gave it exactly the resonance of flowing water. It sounded like a huge singing spring. What's more, having no pine-lyre at this elevation, the shepherd hung it in the branches of an oak. Thus, it was much bigger than usual and it entered the earth more deeply by long radish-like roots.

At the first sounds of music, the whole village cocked its ear, grunted, grabbed pails and tubs, buckets, pitchers, jugs, and rushed toward the valley where the water seemed to be running. But only the wind ran there. They rubbed their eyes, they wondered aloud to each other, they looked right and left without seeing anything, and yet the sound of water was all around them. At the edge of that dry valley, its stones cutting like a hot knife, they got so excited in their desire for live water, that under the sway of that harp, in the supple open air, they began to imitate the movements of swimming, throwing themselves head first onto the rocks, stretching out in the thorns, scraping themselves, scratching themselves, tearing at their goiters, bloody, drunk with despair and desire. Evening came, when the wells were to be opened. They were opened and from them poured, weaker but also blacker, that song of water which came to sing there through the spell of those huge oak roots thrust deep into the rock.

Then there was complete chaos. They thought their water was escaping because some underground river had suddenly given way. Caliste went down into his well to touch the water with his hand and never came up again. And, assembled on the clearing that overlooks the valley of Saint-André, the whole village began to howl at his death like a family of wolves. Our shepherd, having gone too far, made a fast escape into the region of Briançon. Some hunters from Saint-André found the harp, cut the strings, and peace returned with the silence.

So, this is a kind of music that must be measured out, the muted strings not used too much, or just used as a starting point, as a landing for letting the clear notes take wing and fly off. The muted notes have the sadness of doves' songs. The wind is not perfectly round like a iron rod, but made of waves and undulations. It coos and warbles, and if the pleasant notes sound like bird calls, the muted notes weigh on your heart and make the clouds seem like fat pigeons.

Here, the wind harps are at a distance from the clearing of at least a good thousand paces. They must be set up on the ridge to allow them the life of the wind. Then, too, too close up, they would have cut off and killed the narrator's voice. Up above, they are exactly in their place and their distant music is very much the base it must be in the drama.

There are five harps. They are worked by five shepherds and conducted by a sixth who stays there on the stage and whistles through his fingers. Once for silence, twice for sound.

Thus, through the play, the music of these harps unfolds. It doesn't follow the turns in the action. It is distant and monotone like the voice of the world.

THE TYMPON is that flute with nine pipes, the flute of play and of distress. It has one scale and two deep, bass Cs, one at the beginning of the scale, one at the end. These somber notes are always there, ready to sound the alarm at each end of the song.

When all you know is how to play the flute, you only blow into the seven pipes by making the reeds flow before your mouth. That makes a flute song. But, if you've grown accustomed to the tympon from long use and when you truly know how to play it, that adds the leavening to the dough, believe me. Right in the middle of the songs, there's the deep note that sets ringing the whole black basin at the bottom of your heart meant to hold your reserve of tears. Then, you remember in a flash the days of distress. The harsh mountains appear, climbing the sky like she-bears, and the flute song becomes a lyric of life, a verb alive as the day, made at once of joy and sadness.

You can recognize true tympon players by two very specific signs. This is what they are. When a shepherd sits down, the dog comes to lie beside him, the flocks remain a little farther away. If he's a tympon player, every time, you'll see a sheep approach, lay its head on the man's knees and wait for solace. The second sign is that a tympon player, when he's alone, when he's walking alone along his way, he looks behind him ten times, twenty times, to try to see what is back there following him, whose steps he hears in his head.

THE GARGOULETTES are the water flutes. There are two kinds. One is made out of elder wood. They are like pipes. The other is made out of glazed earth. They are like pitchers, and they imitate bird songs.

With little gargoulettes, you can very easily hunt quail or any bird with a trilling song. They imitate them, they call to them, they sound exactly like the female. But the gargoulettes the shepherds use are very big. Their song is at once bird song and horse whinny. Ten men blowing hard into ten gargoulettes can make music that turns you to salt. You have only enough time to raise your eyes to search the sky for a flying winged horse.

The instrument isn't beautiful, just a pipe or a pitcher, and it takes enormous breath to move and puncture water. The players bind their cheeks with a handkerchief or a scarf. Gargoulette music has great power over animals. After just a little, it makes them mad for love, females as well as males. It has the power of springtime. Extending from where a man plays a gargoulette alone on a hill, you can see the rays afterwards, the marks in the grass of all the love struggles of beasts who heard him. They radiate out like the spokes of a wheel.

So there is the whole orchestra. Above, on the ridge, the wind harps, here, next to the stage, the tympon and gargoulette players. This time, there were twelve of them. Everything is invention, even in the music. They don't play traditional tunes. They set off in a flurry, without knowing where they are going, improvising on their own sounds. Before beginning, they say, "With us, you are going to travel far!" And then they play.

So this is what I myself saw in all that. The harps make the sound of the earth which rolls along over the routes of the sky; the tympons, the sound of men, words and steps, and the sound of beating hearts; the gargoulettes, the sound of the beasts who are born, make love, bellow, and die. All that as if, all of a sudden, you had the ears of a god.

As for the actors, first of all, there's the Sardinian. The Sardinian, well, he's at the very center of the stage, and he's the one who begins. The others are there, mixed in with the audience; they aren't designated in advance. They are there just to lean toward their neighbors to tell them, "Wait till you hear what I've got to say!"

The Sardinian cannot go on any longer. He calls, *"The Sea,"* for example. And, all of a sudden, it's someone near you who begins to answer. Everyone shouts to him, "Stand up, stand up!"

He stands up, he goes over, he stands facing the Sardinian, he answers. Only then you know that the one whose velour elbows rubbed against your side was the Sea, was really the sea; he has its voice and soul. When he has finished, he stays there. He has taken his place among the elements. There are even some who won't ever leave their elemental rank; they'll remain all their lives as the the Sea, the River, the Woods. It'll be said that the Sea has claimed his pasture to the left of Seyne, or that the River will come down tomorrow, because one night they were so much that sea and that river that they can never again be called by their father's name, but only by the name of what they are.

The one who has finished speaking remains there with the Sardinian. Another one comes, speaks, then falls silent, and then, he takes the hand of the man who was there before him and he waits. At the end of the play, there is a whole wreath of big homespun men holding each other's hands.

All that happens on stage are steps and greetings, steps to take up one's position, greetings to the Sardinian. As for the rest, it's the words that must show it, and the man who speaks remains still, his arms dangling. There are just two or three places where there is some stage action, always very simple, but occurring at the very height of the pathos. These will be indicated in the play's translation on the following pages.

Written down, the text presents in translation a chaos of bristling and tragic words. Tragic, because I sense all their dense beauty and because I am hopeless before them. The language is the most wild type of sea jargon, made up of Provençal, Genoese, Corsican, Sardinian, Niçoise, Old French, Piedmontese, and words invented on the spot as needed. It is a marvelous instrument for epic drama: cries and howls themselves can be long narratives. The imitative harmony is such that gestures are superfluous as the procession of the planets, the rocking of the sea, the drenched course of the land losing its oceans in space all suddenly appear before the stunned listener. I say this to make your mouth water, but you'll find nothing of all that in my translation. I've done my best to put it into very faulty French, but the language of free men is a leaping beast and, here, I've only forced open the bars of the cage a little.

May I be forgiven.

V

NIGHT. DISTANT SAINT-JEAN FIRES
are eating away at the whole circle of the horizon.

The Mallefougasse plateau. Four fires at the corners of a square of
grazed earth. Next to each flame, a man is standing, a heavy branch of
leaves in his hand. All around this lit clearing, the night, and just at the
edges of the night, like bubbling foam, the shepherds are seated in their
mantles, their overcoats, their big velour jackets.

The Sardinian. He stands up. He looks to the right, and then to
the left, and, at the same time, there is silence to the right and then to the
left.

"So, should we begin?"

Just at that moment, without any other command but that silence,
the wind descends, worked by the harps. The flutes begin to play the
sound of a man who is walking in the sea.

THE SARDINIAN (He moves forward to the middle of the clearing; raises his hand in greeting). *Listen, shepherds:*

The worlds were in the god's net [1] *like tuna in the madrague:*

Flips of the tail and foam; a sound that rang out, expelling the wind from every side.

The god was in the sky up to his knees.

From time to time, he leaned over, he took some sky in his hands. It ran between his fingers. It was white as milk. It was full of creatures like a huge stream of ants. And in it, images became clear and then faded like things in dreams.

The god washed his whole body with the sky. Slowly, to get used to life's cold. He had a sensitive belly. Because everything was created in his belly.

Afterwards, he began to walk into the sky until he was out of his depths, where he could no longer touch, and he began to swim. His huge hand rose and dipped like a spoon; his great feet dug like pickaxes with nails in front. He was followed all along by a swirl of ripped up grasses. After a little while, he was far off over there, no more than an island amidst the spray.

He went off because the beginning was finished.

. .

---

[1] *Net:* I have translated the word *baragne* as *net*, though really it means *hedge*. A flowering hedge, a hedge that the god has sown in the sky and behind which the orchards that never die will turn green. But the end of the sentence allows me to translate *baragne* as *net*. Unless you imagine a hedge of seaweed, a *net* made of huge seaweed from the beginning of the world.

Blood! Clots of blood!

The earth is crouching [2] *in the belly of the sky like a child in its mother.*

It is in the blood and the guts. It hears life, all around, which is roaring like fire.

A blue vein enters its head like a snake. That is how it is filled with its kindness.

A red artery enters its chest. That is how it is filled with its meanness.

It grows thicker. The more it thickens, the more light it has.

Finally, it presses against the portal. It wants to be born. It is heavy with the reason of its seed.

Suddenly, in a jet of fire it is born and it takes off.

This is the earth's youth!

It rolls about in the universe like in the grass. It is all wet with the great blossoming waters. It steams with sweat like a horse who has galloped in the sun.

It trails behind it a lovely odor of milk. You can hear it laughing far off like the sound of nuts cracking.

Its skin is in the process of drying. There are colors that run in circles around it like rainbows. When a patch of its skin is dry, it turns green.

This is the earth's youth!

This is the great Sunday!

All the trees are flowering at the same time. On the water there are wide marshes of blue squash. Rocks pass, full of vines which trail like hair. Little

---

[2] *Crouching:* The text reads: *ajoucado din la mamado dou ciel.* It is as clear-cut as flint, but in French, becomes cloudy. I can see it. I saw it the moment the Sardinian spoke. He didn't make a move. I saw the earth rolled in a ball, knees to belly, head to knees, nose touching chest, crouched like all creatures about to be born.

round stones run under the grass. All the flowers are ruddy with good health. The leaves are thick as your arm. You can hear the fruits which are all ripening together. The big squash float on the sea. Each time the earth moves, the herds of ripe fruit pour from all sides into the folds of the hill. It begins to smell like sugar. The hills drift off very slowly, bent under that great weight. The plains of sand try to lift up their burden of ripe grasses, and then remain completely flat. The mountains weep water. Bitter flowers grow in the bottom of the streams. The rocks stop, ecstatic. That smell of Sunday, which is the smell of tomato soup! [3]

All this time, the Sardinian has remained with his hand raised in greeting and the music has made that sound of water and tumbling earth. You saw the hills walk. You heard their big feet slap in the mud, in the rot of the streams of fruit. Now the narrator lets his raised hand fall. The aeolian harps are all alone trying their hand at the great Sunday. There's the sound of sheets flapping on the clothesline, whirlwinds of swallows, the wind coming from far away in one long slide, now caught in fistfuls in the trees.

A dry music begins, made up of just the tympon, those tries at joy

---

[3] *That smell . . . etc.*: Sunday morning, housewives in little villages make tomato soup. Tomatoes cut in half and seeded—adapted, as they say—water, a cruet of oil, a dish of thin fried onions. All that in the earthenware cookpot on the fire. When it's eleven o'clock, all the cookpots begin to boil and the whole village smells of tomato soup. The shepherd had arrived in the morning and, all heavy with fatigue and dust, he sleeps under the plane trees. That smell of tomato soup is the smell of Sunday for him, of wonderful Sunday, when you have the day off, a house, a clean table, a cool hearth, washed, blue of the blue of stone and lavender in the shelves of the wardrobe; wonderful Sunday when your wife is ready to stretch out beside you, with all her flesh, when you're no longer a shepherd, that sailor of the land, that runner between ports of call, that wanderer. . . . All that a dream, because the shepherd is alone under the plane trees and the village belongs to others.

along the scale and the loud notes sounding like calls. With a wing beat of his arms, this is what the Sardinian did: he changed character. He is no longer the anonymous narrator, he is the earth-narrator. He is the Earth. From now on, he is going to tell us of his anxiety; the drama opens.

THE SARDINIAN. *The great grasses have eaten all my strength. I realized this because I wanted to leap into the sky and I couldn't, and I remain stuck here, powerless.*

I've been too lax with all these beautiful trees. Already everything that ran and danced over me, the hills and the mountains, and the high rocks, everything has stopped, hindered by forests and undergrowth.

Oh! I wanted to go much farther and I couldn't, and I turn, and I turn again, but it's all clamped together in me by hooked roots. I'm like a moldy apple.

The summers came upon me like huge bees, and they sapped my moisture. They didn't budge. They were upon me, wings open.

I knew it: I had seen the great marshes of squash withering on the waters. The squash drifted off and then, suddenly, they plunged into the water's depths. And then, other times, I saw bubbles rise, and then, other times, all the water moved.

The summers' swarm drank up nearly all the lovely depth of the water. And then, I saw the great serpent's back.

There is that great serpent who is a creature of the mud. Then there are those who have four feet and are made according to the model of the sky because they have teats to drink from. There is one of those who is almost nothing but a mouth; it swallows huge platefuls of pines and birches and whole cherry orchards along with the ground underneath, covered with grass and shadows. There are many others, too.

And I was lighter with grass, but I was heavier with meat and I sank into the sky like a lead weight because all these beasts were stepping over each other, were mounting each other, making little ones who were making little ones.

And then, one fine moment, I stopped drifting because the beasts began to eat meat. There were some who ate grass and others who ate the ones who ate the grass. And that created balance.

And I am in balance.

But, now, I feel this balance coming all undone again, and it's swaying. Something else has happened. Oh, what a worry it is to have skin and a belly!

I'm very nervous because of that one, I've heard he wants to take charge.

And yet, he is small; I raise and lower my eyebrows and I widen my eyes, and I turn them about, and I turn them about again. I see nothing.

Nevertheless, this thread of balance is swaying. I have to ask . . .

Since he became the earth-narrator, the Sardinian was clearly hurrying to reach those words by which the drama opens. At first, he added a bit of polish. Then, he abandoned his images as he went along. He spoke of the summers like bees. I saw the Sardinian again a little later. He told me very beautiful things about the summer: the summer that alights on us like a swarm; the summer that covers the land with a hot flayed skin.

Moreover, the whole circle of shepherds had begun to talk and near me I heard repeated "And you, what will you say?" After "*I have to ask,*" the Sardinian stood for a moment not saying anything. All the music stopped.

THE SARDINIAN (He calls). *The Sea!*

Nothing. Silence. Shepherds who squeeze close to each other like sheep who are afraid.

THE SARDINIAN (in another, natural, voice). *So, there's no one to do the sea?*

Over there, in back, there's a group where a little dispute is bubbling and you can hear "Go on," "Go on," in low voices.

He goes forward.

It's a short, fat shepherd. He takes two or three steps, then he turns around and flings his big felt hat to his friends. He is bald, with two little wings of white hair above his ears.

I learned afterwards that his name is Glodion and that he's from Le Bachas, a country of complete wilderness: nothing but stones, nothing but stones and thistle.

GLODION. *I'm the Sea!*

He and the Sardinian face each other like two men who are going to dance.

THE SARDINIAN. *Sea.*
  Tell me if you know what is worrying me.
  Look at me swinging to and fro.
  Who knows where I am going to go now?
  Things went better for me when I was young.
  But then my worries started.
  And I am much more afraid of what is coming than of what has been.

GLODION. *What is it you want me to say?*

THE SARDINIAN. *Tell me if you have seen man.*

GLODION. *Man?*

Stop swinging me from side to side for a bit. You are hurling me into the mountains with the goats; you are throwing me from the flat sand as far as the eye can see, all the way to where the monkeys live.

Wait!

I don't have time to look around.

Man?

You mean that fish who is all planted with grass like a big meadow and whom all my purple rage can't budge, and who sleeps stretched out on the grill of a thousand of my waves?

THE SARDINIAN. *Maybe.*

What does this fish do?

You say that he sleeps on a thousand waves, so he is big?

GLODION. *Yes.*

It's because he's too big that he sleeps. What use would it be for him to go anywhere? With one stroke, he's on this side, with another stroke, he's on the other. He is just one big pocket of skin. When it's full of water, he sinks into my shade, toward the coolness because it's hot. When it's full of air, he climbs back up, he is over me like a meadow of grass. Big pieces of ice come to plant themselves in him, and then they melt there.

THE SARDINIAN. *No.*

That's not the one who makes me nervous, then, if he only sleeps. Look harder.

GLODION. *What is it I feel in me?*

It's anger or maybe it's great distress that twists me in its pains?

The wind suddenly put its foot in the middle of me and that's what made me leap up to the clouds.

Oh, this anger, you don't know how bad it can be, because it's anger against nothing.

It swells in me like a bad hurt; it makes a kind of heavy pus that sleeps for a long time deep inside me.

Then, all of a sudden:

With one of those swings that you make me take when you throw me against my shores, this anger rips me apart.

And then, first of all, I become full of huge flowers like the wide open flowers of carrots.

I swell like abscesses on bad meat.

I explode, I groan, I weep, I gnash my huge sand teeth.

I twist and turn and I endure the great death.

THE SARDINIAN. *That's because the cold despair of the whole universe has rested upon you.*

It's because he's unhappy that the god made the world.

He wanted to get out of himself and each time he thought of something, the forms began to clarify everything he thought.

Thus, I was conceived in the belly of the sky, and you, sea, you were that side of me that rested against the sky at that place in its flank where it keeps its bile and its bitterness.

And you became the bile and the bitterness of the world.[4] *But look again and tell me . . .*

---

[4] Here, in the two speeches of Glodion and the Sardinian, we have the very model of the improvisation that makes every performance different from all others. Glodion clearly and

GLODION. *What?*

Why should I tell you and what should I tell you . . . ?

All this bitterness is exactly what I feel, and I would like to scatter it into the whole universe, and for the sky, that other ocean that is above me, to become bitter waves to its very depths and to go off tossing salt on the beaches of the stars.

Earth, do you remember the time of your youth, when you ran, water squash, in the great prairie of the night, and how, with my depths, I soaked the wide route?

In those quarters of the sky where, alone, we could live: me, the sea, them, the mountains, our immense life which goes from one side of life to the other, without stopping, slowly, slowly, slowly.

And you desired to carry more rapid lives, and you rolled over the blue slopes, and you crossed the quarter of fruits, and you were in the sky like a ball of sugar, like a ripe melon.

I heard you laughing.

But the slope threw you into the great region of beasts and there you are all covered with that mildew of blood, and there you are getting nervous over a new animal, and there you are like a girl who's rolled in the hay with men and who's looking at her belly.

THE SARDINIAN. *There!*

Calm down, Sea!

---

purposefully distanced himself from the subject to speak of the sea's anger. It became a duel between him and the Sardinian. We clapped for the lines on the sea's anger. We clapped for the Sardinian's lines in response. Often, within the drama's text, we will find this dueling between the narrator and the actor. Fundamentally, I believe that the whole interest for the shepherds lies in this battle of words. The Sardinian interrogates and tries to trip up the actor, who responds by slipping out of his way, as in a round of wrestling, and grabbing a handful of flesh. Victory goes to whoever will throw the other into the dust.

Let that high tongue of water that you raise to the sky come down. Make yourself flat.

Who knows what life the god has imagined for me?

Who can know in advance all the forms⁵ which are still only air waiting ready in the darkness?

This course of mine, it was written in the stars. I was delighted with the fruits; I listened to the lowing of the beasts and now, there before me, opening wide, is this region of man, and my course can't avoid it.

Because the god has bound into my flesh this curse: the capacity to produce.⁶

Make yourself flat, Sea, make yourself smooth and sleep.

I am going to ask the Mountain.

Mountain!

As before, silence. But this time, someone is ready, stands up, and waits. He respects the order of the play. You have to leave time for the aeolian harp players above to understand by the whistle that the sea's scene is over.

Besides, that sound of the sea which continues to diminish, and then falls still, coincides with the gestures of Glodion the shepherd. He parts with the Sardinian, takes two steps backwards, and remains there.

One gargoulette, just one, very slowly plays the song of "*O bellos montagnos.*" It makes it into a kind of formidable monster, full of waterfalls, ice collapsing, the sound of the north wind, grinding, spitting,

---

⁵ *forms:* dolls

⁶ *This curse . . .* etc.: literally, this manure which makes me create things.

and it all ends in silence into which pipes a little tune from the tympon, only the scale notes, the little streamer of music that floats on the lips of the shepherd walking ahead of the sheep.

THE MOUNTAIN (The man moves forward, salutes, stands facing the Sardinian as if for a contredanse). *Earth!*

Are you worried?

Because someone came to look in at the gate and then, when you turned around to see, you saw only quick movements as they hid.

And now, in the great afternoon, you sense a presence over there behind the pillars, and everything is turning cloudy around you as in a stream when a big fish dies at the bottom, disturbing the mud.

And you call out, and you ask . . .

Earth, I don't know!

I don't know, but I can feel your anxiety moving under my feet.

I expected it.

For a long time, I had my pasture of solitude and silence and already I was bound by the weight of all the grasses, the weight of trees, this mud of big, rotten fruits.

I learned to know the sound of the life of the plants. One day, a shadow came over me, a cold shadow that crossed me slowly.

It was the shadow of a bird.

And under it, I was colder than under the shadow of the night.

It was then that I felt your anxiety moving.

It was then I understood from the taste of the sky that we had passed the threshold that opens onto the region of men.

Listen to me.

I can no longer move and I am too high to see below.

But I have sent someone to explore it.
He already left a good while ago; he won't be long in coming back.

Without another call, a man stood up, not very far from the spot where I am and where I'm scribbling this down. Césaire let out an "Eh, look!" and I felt Barberousse against me turn to look. Césaire's girl leans the whole weight of her hand on my knee and stands up. I remain seated; I don't want to upset my writing board and my papers and, in the movement of the girl's head, in her gaze, I follow, from below, the one who moves forward into the play. I hear what someone says to him: "You, who are you?" He answers, "You'll see." He has entered the stage area; I can see him. He is tall and thin, all shaven. He has a slight limp.

THE MAN. *Here I am. I'm back. I am the River.*[7]

GLODION–THE SEA (who until then remained motionless, moves forward in greeting). *Ah! The one I was waiting for!*
For a long time I've been hearing you rolling in the fields and the marshes.

---

[7] *I am the River:* There was an "Ah!" There was no more music, except the sound of the aeolian harps. Regarding the importance of the distant instruments in this type of performance: they don't participate in the emotion produced by sudden dramatic action, and from them, music flows continually. Thus, the drama is always in suspension. The River and the Mountain had come to an agreement before the performance of this scene which left the Sardinian a little disconcerted for the moment. We immediately see the Sea take advantage of this to attack the narrator with a new improvisation. Thus we can understand the mechanism for continual renewal in this oral drama.

The narrator—here, it's the Sardinian—is like the holder of a cup, a title, a torch. Everyone conspires to unseat him. He is alone against all the others.

Finally, here you are with your dead trees, your dead beasts.

You have crushed a lot of things to get here!

Ah! Earth! If you believe that one, we're not done laughing yet.

He drags himself along beating his head everywhere he goes like a blind snake.

He has knocked down hills, he has slashed the great skin of grass. He's a carrier of dead things.

He only knows reflections.

THE SARDINIAN (He raises his hand. There is no more music except the sound of the harps). *Don't say anything bad about reflections!*

Or about death!

The universe is a globe of reflections.

GLODION–THE SEA. *Yes!*

But this river that's before you and that comes to tell you: "I'm the one who knows!"

I'm telling the truth, now: he doesn't know the worth of reflections, and he takes them and leaves them. He doesn't carry them.

THE SARDINIAN. *He carries them.*

In a thousand times a thousand years they will find in his mud the reflection of that little willow leaf which is mirrored this day.

That reflection which is like a seal in wax, like a good or bad thought that leaves its mark.

THE RIVER. *Why try to debate with the Sea?*

Look at the beasts: they come forward, they sniff, they smell this odor of salt; then they turn tail and run off in the other direction.

You know what I call her?
The sweaty one.
There she is with her big breasts, leaping and sweating.
But me, the beasts come to me, and they drink.

GLODION–THE SEA *They drink!*
I know.
I heard the cries of those you forced to drink in the recesses of a high hill. And then, I heard the silence.

THE RIVER. *We have ways that are written from eternity in the script of the stars.*
And we have our work all laid out.
Do you want the world to shift places because the does and the stags are there in the cul-de-sac of the rocks?
Yes, they drank, and beyond their thirst.
But it was decreed that I had to push my head against that rock and make that pocket of earth into a great whirlpool.
That was done.
What are a thousand stags in the wheels of the world?

THE SARDINIAN. *Tell me, River.*
Did you encounter man?

THE RIVER. *I encountered what he left.*
Here it is:
You know that I'm made of sky; you can believe me. In descending from the mountain, I got tangled up in a large forest and for a long time I looked for my

proper course, and I slept there, laid flat, under the trees, and I was eaten by the big green flies.

There, I remained a long time, my muscles building up for nothing. Everyday, my flesh swelled a little more all along the length of my skin, but that was all.

The trees lay over me; long grasses pushed through me as through a dead snake and I began to smell bad.

It was a mountain forest and, from one place, it leaned over the steps of the mountain.

When I learned that, in the fold of the grass, I inflated my head. It became round and glistening, and all my weight, all my strength inflated my head. It became like one of those big drops which are the stars; it weighed down, it tore itself away, and finally it made the leap toward that wide hillocky plain, greenish-gray as an old cauldron, and my whole body followed.

During the leap, I saw the great herds of beasts running and, there in front, a beast who walked on its two hind feet.

And I threw out my huge arms from all sides and I ripped out great trees by the fistful, and I saw wolves who climbed into the oaks and chamois who ran in the flat grass with the regular trot of horses, heavy bears who leaped, like bubbles, over the marshes, mares and forests of foals so thick you could only see their backs and heads, and all of that trembling like leaves in the wind.

And I forced myself to catch up with a wide forest that fled before me. There were branched stags and so many does they seemed like clouds pushed by the wind. At the end of the world there was a high red hill and it barred the route and I hit it with all the strength of my white forehead and my idea.

It was to this that the Sea referred earlier with her bitter words, typical of those who have green lips and tongues of salt. It's true, I made the great forest of stags drink, but listen, Sea, and learn, Sea, what the law is, and the good balance:

They turned toward me, and head to head, we battled.

Me, with my soft blue head. Them, with their heads of stone and those pointed branches that spread out above them like the branches of oaks.

And I began to climb over the does and the fawns, softer than the limp new branches of the fig tree and I packed all that under me till I felt the quivering of its blood.

Finally, from the height of this platform, I attacked the stags and I retreated, then I hit with my whole head, and, each time, I was torn open, and the water ran between the deers' antlers and they shook their heads with anger, and they bared their teeth and bit into me, and everything was a chaos of spray and sweat.

And then, I felled them like huge trees, and in my depths, they became mud.

That's the law.

Am I the one who will teach you, Sea, what mud is, you who saw your bitter greenness flower with life, at the time when life descended upon the earth like a seed, at the time when earth entered through that door of the sky into the regions where life is permitted. You who saw that bitter mud of your shores lift like the back of a serpent and toss to bits all the creatures of the world .[8]

Earth!

It was one evening.

And I had no more anger, no more fight, and I was flowing.

It was evening; in peace I crossed a large blue forest and the whole sky sang our two songs.

---

[8] For some time now, the lame one who is the River has been speaking, stirred by the trances that inhabit and agitate him. He makes gestures; he moves his arms about.

I learned afterwards that he is very famous among the shepherds for his gushing inspiration which bursts forth on all sorts of occasions when he is alone with people of the mountains. I have two of his poems: "Mary-Mother's Breast" (a hymn for his church) and "My Valley Under the Oaks" (a song).

On one of my sloping banks, there were the tracks of beasts. And, in the midst of them, the tracks of man.

THE SARDINIAN (He raises his hand to stop the cripple). *Stop, River, stop!*

Ah!

Repeat what you said: the tracks of man were in the midst of the tracks of the beast?

THE RIVER. *Yes.*

Wide tracks that went off into the woods.

THE SARDINIAN. *I'm lost, that's my death.*

That's the death of me, the living earth!

No longer will I be this big beast sprawling in the sky.

But I'll be put to pasture like the cow.

If man has become the master of the beasts.

Speak!

THE RIVER. *I don't know.*

I saw that image of feet that pierced the mud here and there and entered the woods.

But I couldn't follow.

Ask the Tree.

. .

So here we are in pursuit of man. Here we are in pursuit of that primary position held by the Sardinian.

For right now, I'm not going to translate the rest of the play. I only wanted to give a long series of scenes to show how the serpentine action unfolds. Furthermore, it does not form a whole, a round fruit well sealed off from the sky all around, but it is, on the contrary, like a soft fig, too ripe on one side, its honey dripping gold, and on the other side, bitter and creamy with the milk of the tree, because the shepherds don't all have the same poetic powers, and in the best flow, there is some water without taste.

As for the Sardinian's prime place, it will be threatened throughout by the Sea. Glodion will have his say from time to time and each time, it will brutally interrupt the Sardinian's inspiration. So that finally he will be told:

O Sea, made jealous by all your salt;
Of all this salt that burns your skin,
Jealous of all the greenness.
Leave us in peace.
It would be a beautiful world indeed if it was made up only of you,
We would be soft as an egg without a shell,
And you would lose your fish in the sky
All along your course.

To tell the truth, as for the Sardinian's primary position, that power that launches the drama like gunpowder, no one wants to see it taken away from the one who holds it. Except for the cripple who did the River, the other shepherds are not up to it, and never will anyone say anything that can compete with the opening monologue, which I call "the birth and youth of the earth." Even the cripple has faults. He can only improvise in a trance, in a sort of fever that makes his eyes glow in a wind that thrashes him about, limbs strewn. The Sardinian remains motionless as a column. He only moves for the greetings. From this stillness flows a great nobility and when, at the end of the drama, remaining alone, he makes a few essential gestures, they go to the height of tragedy in a single bound.

So here is the pursuit of man.

The Tree arrives. It says what it sees from the top of its head:

From the shores of that river
to the red tree
and beyond more than twenty hills which mount each other like rams and
ewes.

It indicates man's route, that track in the grass: *like the slime of a slug.* But from the red tree on, it loses sight of it.

But, there's the Wind and here it comes with a leap. The Wind, at the end of one of its courses, has encountered man and has accompanied him because it has found him:

. . . not at all thorny
and supple as silk, and very light on the two springs of his legs.
And his arms are like two wings that tickle without beating me.

It accompanied man in a strange search, full of leaps and slides flat on the stomach, of breathless races. Finally, the man found what he was looking for: his female. She was there:

naked, hidden in the grass like a frog.

And there was the chase, angular and quick as a flash of lightning, and then the man seized the female. And there, the wind saw nothing more because the two bodies pulled each other down under the shelter of the bushes, in the grass.

The Sardinian calls the Grass.

The Grass has seen it all and tells it all. It tells it, without fear of words and things. It's all men here, and what took place in the shelter of the bushes is the act of life, as simple, as pure as the swelling of a cloud.

The Grass uses a beautiful word to speak of the man's actions; he uses "*pastéjavo*" which means, "he kneaded the dough."

And the Grass saw the slow life of the couple and those hours of dreaming in which, more than the beasts, these new creatures remained there, motionless, and:

went off into the depths of the hour
on a serpent's back.
One day:

Then, from each side of his female
he hollowed two great streams.
And there she was like a spring,
there she was like a fountain of children;
and the children flowed from her like the stream from the fountain.
And the last ones are still there crawling close to her like fresh nuts, while, already on their two feet the first ones have arrived at the edge of the forest, before the world, and in their thick hands, they carry the fruit of fire.

The Grass' account was the peak of the drama. If someday the Sardinian must be defeated, I hope—and he himself hopes—that his replacement will be the shepherd who spoke the words of the Grass for us.

When he had finished speaking, the Sardinian approached him, his hand extended. They shook hands two or three times and the Sardinian said, "Bravo! . . ."

This shepherd is an assistant for the herd for which the Sardinian is the master.

After the Grass came the Rain. That one told us all it knew of man's exterior:

Because I've encountered him many times!
And because there is not a fold, not a groove in his body which I have not kissed.
He has:

A head like that stone which makes fire
and the power that makes hillocks of his chest and his legs and his arms, it comes from within his head.
And the female:

Some are as lively as little mice
and they are like the fruit of the thyme, that little green star soft with honey, but with a bitterness that swells the tongue.
I run over her as over the naked hills but I never go farther than her belly because a fire is hidden there, hotter than the fire of the sun.
The one that will tell us of man's interior is the Cold. That one has entered, has gone within to the inside of man, all the way to:

That place where life and death are welded together: to that welded place where there is a roll of flesh like in those earthworms which have been cut and which have grown back together.

Inside man it has seen:

Stars and suns, and huge shooting stars which bring fire to all the corners and the beautiful shepherd's stars which climb in the calm of peace.

A vast sky, all blue like the sky of earth, with a sun, storms, and great, spiteful flashes of lightening.

And quantities of stars that go off in all directions, herds here, herds there, in the great turmoil of joy, when he approaches his female.

The Cold has seen the whole interior of man like a sky full of powers. The Beast who comes next will say that he is:

like a pot full of honey which overflows, and which nourishes with its overflow a whole tribe of flies.

For us, he is like a great tree we desire after a long trot in the sun.

He is like the grass slope for the feet of those who have climbed.

He is fresh water;

he is the spring.

He is the great palm, the beautiful stream, the cool leaves, and all of these together.

It will speak of that seduction that is in man's eyes and it will tell the Earth the great secret, the beasts' great hope:

Do you know why we are afraid, Earth?

Do you know why we are wild,

why we listen to the wind and sniff the dust?
It's because we feel ourselves carried by you, crossing the sky at a horrible
speed.
And, he who has come,
we've read in his eyes that he doesn't see your life, Earth.
We've read in his eyes tranquillity and peace, and that's why we love him.

And then, from there, the play will make two leaps that will carry it to
the end.

First, a long monologue from the Sardinian. The nine shepherds,
who were the Sea, the Mountain, the River, the Tree, the Wind, the
Grass, the Rain, the Cold, the Beast, are still and silent. They hold one
another's hands and they form a horseshoe around the Sardinian.

The Sardinian gives us the final word on Earth's anxiety and why it
has questioned so hungrily. It knows, it recognizes the danger that
threatens it. If man becomes the master of beasts, it, the Earth, is lost:

I see him, already, there ahead of the great herd.
He will walk along at his easy pace
and behind him, there you will all be.
And then, he will be the master.
He will command the forests.
He will make you camp out in the mountains,
He will make you drink the rivers.
He will make the sea advance or retreat, by merely moving the flat of his
hand.

A moment of silence, then the Earth begins to look around:

The great reflection of all images.

And as it reads the hidden writing, its voice reassures and prophesies.

The great barrier!
It will always be between beast and man, that high barrier black as night, high as the sun.
And were all the pity piled up in your skin, you would never be able to make it run from you or make the beasts drink from it.
You will never jump the barrier and enter on equal footing the great forest of the beast's reflections.
You will not look at the same reflections.
You will see the trees from the other side, and the others, they will see another side of the trees.
And all that, because I am going to be harsh with you, harsh and spiteful, and I am going to think about my spitefulness.

~ ~ ~ ~ ~ ~ ~ ~ ~ ~ ~ ~ ~ ~ ~ ~ ~ ~

You will be the master of gold and stones, but without understanding the stones, you will massacre them with your trowel and your pick.
And as for gold, made of light, you will guard it in the dark stench of your mouth.

~ ~ ~ ~ ~ ~ ~ ~ ~ ~ ~ ~ ~ ~ ~ ~ ~ ~

You will make yourself aids with iron, bolts and hinges.
But you will be obliged to offer your head and your heart to all your machines and you will become as evil as the iron and the jaws of the hinge.

Then, the Earth is delighted and begins to laugh from all its volcanoes.

At that moment that the drama takes its second leap and the Sardinian ends with a simple gesture. He sheds his Earth character, and he again becomes what he is: a man. More than that: a shepherd. More than that: a master of beasts, one of those masters that the earth dreads. And that is the truth.

He takes three steps, he disengages himself from the semi-circle of the elements. Slowly, he kneels; he lies down belly to the earth; he embraces the earth with his outspread arms. We hear him say:

Earth!
Earth!
We are here, it's us, the masters of beasts!
We are here, it's us, the first men!
There are some among us who have kept their hearts pure.
We are here.
Do you feel our weight?
Do you feel how we weigh more than the others?
They are here, those men who see the two sides of the tree and the inside of the stone, those who walk in the thinking of the beast as in the wide meadows of Dévoluy above the well-loved grasses.
They are here, those who have leapt the barrier!

He remains for a brief moment not saying anything, waiting for a response that doesn't come and he cries his great cry of defiance:

Do you hear, Earth?
We are here, it's us, the shepherds!

All the instruments fall still at the same time. Silence!
You can hear the fires crackle.
And it's over.

. .

I HAVE not spoken of the music for some time. Never did it stop playing a part in the drama. Never did it stop being another drama beside
the drama, full of reflections, in which leaves became foliage and the
image of one hill became the rolling sea of the whole hilly country.
During the last scene, when the narrator kneels and lies down on the
earth, the most beautiful song of rejoicing breaks out, the most beautiful song of the world, the most charged with hope, but the task that I
had imposed upon myself, which was to capture it word for word, to
follow the text with all my attention, prevented that swaying abandon
which alone could have carried me through the images of that music.
Nevertheless, I still have a few of them under my eyelids; they are there,
as hard as grains of sand or as soft as tears.

WE UNTIED the mare. Already, the herds were heading off; already, far
off, above, in the Sisteron passes, the tide of beasts sounded like the
great rolling waters.

Césaire went off to find water for the mare to drink. The little sorceress lay down in the bottom of the cart. The two of us, Barberousse and I,

stayed there, with no will to do anything, bruised and softened from all sides, bathed in the bath of life like that god at the beginning who washed himself with the sky, and we watched the trembling lantern of dawn lighting up.

The aeolian harp players passed close to us, returning from their heights. They spoke loudly, with voices full of young laughter. Barberousse recognized among them the voice of a friend and cried, "Greetings, Boromé!"

"And who is that?" said Boromé, stopping himself mid-conversation.

Then he moved forward, recognized Barberousse, and they embraced heartily, beard to beard. Despite his laugh, Boromé was also an old shepherd, gray-haired, skin all hollowed by the scars of time.

"You get the smallest share," I said to him.

He answered me, "Why is that?"

"Because you harp players are so far away, up above, and you can't hear the beautiful speeches."

He said to me, "No, don't think that. Shares! Who's to say who gets the biggest share! We are alone on top of the hill, with our sounds. We say what we want to say, without words.

"We look at the sky. And just now, high up in the middle of the night, I saw a great serpent of stars! It's enough to imagine."

Appendix

A complete translation of Scene IV of the Shepherds' Play

THE GREAT SILENCE HAS COME. The narrator is without words, there, between the fires. He has just spoken the words which must bring about man's birth. The play needs a man with his terrors, one of those from before the waters, wide eyes trembling like bees, mouth open over his ecstasy, his fear and his drool. And if such a man is present, it's only by chance. It takes a shepherd with a heavy heart to do this man, and you don't always find him because that heaviness of heart (as Barberousse explained to me) comes from the sediment misfortune leaves in man. Many misfortunes, much sediment, and a heavy heart.

Great silence. Here and there, a ram's bell rings. A shepherd stands up. He doesn't move forward into the stage clearing. He remains in the middle of the audience. The narrator has heard the noise of the shepherd who has stood. He turns his way. He greets him in silence, raising his left hand. The shepherd greets the narrator, also raising his left hand, and then, shrugging his shoulders, he sheds his heavy homespun cloak.

THE MAN (He cries slowly, in a high-pitched voice). *Lord, I am naked, and you have tossed out handfuls of fleece and foliage.*

Lord, I am naked, and you have given the claws from your hands and the toenails from your feet to the beasts.

Lord, I am naked, and you have given me a poor heart all sick with wind like the bell of little flowers.

THE NARRATOR (who plays the role of the world. He speaks in a solemn voice and a muted gargoulette that accompanies him lowers the tone further still). *And man will be upon me like a mountain among mountains; he will flow with forests, he will walk, dressed in all the hair of the beasts.*

He will be the lion among lions: the odor from his mouth will terrify the lambs and fawns, and even the birds high in the air, those who are like the bell of little flowers.

He will be the summit among summits: his head will climb to meet the stars and with his blue gaze he will count the stars, like sheep in the folds of the pastures.

THE MAN. *Lord, I am naked, and your pity has bent over the water and not over me. And you have given the water, with its beautiful green skin, that garb of grasses and trees, and you have told that skin that it would make the spray, and your sun lights that spray with a higher joy than the most wide open flowers.*

Lord, I am naked, and your pity has bent over the water and not over me. And you have given the water a wide body that strikes the mountains and the sands, flesh that runs through claws, a depth in which sleeps silence more beautiful than woman. You have made water the never wounded, the forever living, unique, eternal, without pain or demise.

Lord, I am naked, and your pity has bent over the water and not over me. And you have given the water the joy of fits of rage, and you have given it that honey which is a song, a flow beneath the grass. Ah! Lord, they are under the willows, and the swaying of the brambles, so beautiful, those songs, so pure, so right, so round with the lovely line that closes the world, that nothing is left to me but the freedom of groaning.

THE NARRATOR. *He will walk over the waters.*

He will have the round seas crushed under the arches of his feet like rotten fruit.

He will go off over the waters at his easy pace.

He will have wide wooden shoulders and he will swing his wooden shoulders walking over the waters.

He will make himself wings with the white grasses, his chest will be like a wishbone from a goshawk and he will go off over the waters to meet death full of images.

THE MAN. *Lord, I am naked, and you have bound me wrist and ankle and you have thrown me to the cold earth like a kid to be slaughtered.*

Lord, I am naked, and you have shown me your wide hands full of salt, and you whistled between your lips as if to call me, and I followed you as far as the salt stones⁹ because I was hungry for that good bitterness.

Lord, I am naked, and you have kicked me in the stomach to push me away, and I haven't had my share of that good bitterness. I haven't had my share of salt, while the whole world lapped all around the salt stones.

THE NARRATOR. *Around him, there are good trees and grass as thick as clouds, and he lives in a long morning. The flowers answer each other from hillside to hillside and on the hills, there are flights of pigeons like smoke from dry wood.*

And there all around him are the beech trees and the durmast oaks, the apple trees, with apples green as worlds.

---

9 *Pierre d'assalier:* In the high pastures, the shepherds go find flat rocks and they line them up in the grass. These are the salt stones. Every night, the shepherds pour four or five handfuls of rough gray salt on these flat rocks. It's for the nursing ewe; it's for the trembling young lamb; it's for the good sheep huddled with cold or the one who has a thorn in its foot; it's a consolation and a remedy; it thickens their fat and makes the beast's heart a little more solid. Who can know the sheeps' suffering in the high meadows? Who can know? I have seen some of them who, with their stone brows, stood up to a terrible twilight, heavy with despair. Oh! that light, and that air, and the dark scent of the earth wet with crushed grass: all that truly erases hope; all that truly erases hope to the end of all time. And they were there, and they gazed without blinking, and I saw that the night rose in those heads like water in a bowl at the fountain. And then, in the end, they swung their heads in despair and slowly went off toward the salt stones. I saw them in the blurred remains of the day; I saw them before I myself sank into a horror of despair; with great strokes of their tongues, they licked what was left of the salt on the stone.

These salt stones are lined up in the grass. You can see them from far off. A sheep who sees a salt stone doesn't get lost; it will return to the pasture as if drawn by a rope. At those times when the mountain is deserted and the herds have gone below, you can find solitary salt stones here and there. They are polished like worshipped rocks, all the rough edges have been licked, worn smooth by tongues and lips.

And there is the beautiful sun, flowing free like water, spreading under his feet.

Man, listen to this great song of all creation, of all the living, of all that surrounds you. If you walk, everything walks beside you and your route is followed by herds of spine-swaying hills, shaking their springs like bells, rubbing the thick wool of their woods under your feet. If you stop, listen to the fish that jump in the lake; listen to that flat water that comes to sing, lapping at the willows; listen to the beautiful wind resting in the apple trees; listen to the beautiful wind rearing up under the pines like a horse in fresh oats.

THE MAN. *Lord, Lord, I am bound like the beasts and you have tied my elbows behind my back, and my heels are bound, and my chest is offered up, and here is my neck, bare and hot, offered up, with all its poor life running up and down it like a mad little mouse.*

Lord, Lord, I am bound like the beasts, and I am waiting for your knife, and I can only see a bit of the sky, and maybe your knife is going to come from that corner I can't see, which is hidden behind the big star polished like a ram's brow.

Lord, Lord, I am bound like the beasts and here is my neck, offered up.

THE NARRATOR. *Man! Freer than smoke itself, if only you understood your great liberty!*

Oh! Starved for air, oh seeker of the beyond, who are you to have looked into the great face of the depths of the sky, which is made up of clouds in play?

Your feet, your hands, your eyes, your mouth, the whole circle of your thighs, and the whole circle of your arms, and the sharpness of your belly, and the flat of your hand, all of that is besieged with happiness; happiness lies upon it like the oceanic sea on its base of mountain. And you shut yourself in like clay and you search for happiness within yourself.

Open yourself!

Here you are crossed by the suns and the clouds; here you are traveled by wind. Listen to the beautiful wind that dances over your blood as over mountain lakes; listen to the way it makes the beautiful sound of its depths ring out!

Here you are bristling with sun, free to walk in the thorns, and the thorns break under your heel, and your head is buzzing like a nest of wasps.

Here you are all light with clouds, and you leap into the sky, and you leap through the beautiful waves of the sky like an eagle.

Open yourself!

Obey the law of the trees and the beasts. Harden your brow; face things with the forehead of a ram. The circle of your arms, see, it is exactly the size of your female. It slips into those two beautiful valleys that she has above her hips. It flows into those valleys of her flesh like waterfalls into the folds of mountains. Your hand is hollowed to the exact roundness of her breasts. You are like the great shore bordering the sea, and the sea surrounds your promontories and enters your bays, and the law of the worlds fuses you to your female like it fused the sea to its shore.

Open yourself!

The highest meadows will enter into you with their colors and smells; with the shaft of oats, with the swaying of grasses ripe with grain, with the heavy "yes" of the gentians who say "yes" all day long nodding their big yellow heads up and down in the wind.

The spring that lies under there under the chestnut tree trembling under the dead leaves like a sensitive little creature, feel it! It has just opened itself above your heart, in your flesh, yes, in your warm flesh the source of water has just opened itself; it runs over your heart as over a stone in the forest, and each drop is like a drum beat, and everything sounds in you, and everything resounds in you from the little cord which makes your fingers move to the big nerve which gives